A Promise Is Forever

ROBIN JONES GUNN

BETHANY HOUSE PUBLISHERS
MINNEAPOLIS, MINNESOTA 55438

A Promise is Forever
Revised edition 1999
Copyright © 1994, 1999
Robin Jones Gunn

Edited by Janet Kobobel Grant
Cover illustration and design by Lookout Design Group, Inc.

Published by Bethany House Publishers
11400 Hampshire Avenue South
Bloomington, Minnesota 55438

Bethany House Publishers is a division of
Baker Publishing Group, Grand Rapids, Michigan.

Printed in the United States of America

Library of Congress Cataloging-in-Publication Data
Gunn, Robin Jones, 1955–
    A promise is forever / by Robin Jones Gunn.
       p. cm. — (The Christy Miller Series ; 12)
    Summary: Eighteen-year-old Christy Miller goes on a missionary trip
to Europe with her friends Katie and Doug and is reunited with her old
boyfriend Todd.
    ISBN 1-56179-733-2
    [1. Missionaries—Fiction. 2. Christian life—Fiction.
3. Friendship—Fiction.] I. Title. II. Series:Gunn,RobinJones,1955–
Christy Miller Series ; 12.
PZ7.G972Pr   1994   94–19929
[Fic]—dc20   CIP
                                                     AC

04 05 06 07 08 09 10 / 17 16 15 14 13 12 11 10 9 8

To Ross, young Ross, and Rachel,
my wonderful family.
I hold the three of you in my heart—forever.

Contents

Acknowledgments

Writing this series has been a great joy to me. Many "peculiar treasures" have joined me in this adventure, and I'd like to say thanks to all of you.

Thanks to my friends at Focus: Janet, Beverly, Rolf, Al, Gwen, Nancy, Bruce, and David.

Thanks to my friends in Great Britain: Noel, Linda, Andrea, Robin, Charles, Jennie, Avril, Ruby, Norman, Lynn, and Mark.

Thanks to my friends in other parts of Europe: Merja, Satu, Leo, Mike, Stephanie, Jakobs, Vija, Mary, Donna, and Wendy Lee.

Thanks to all the young princesses around the world who have become friends with Christy Miller and have written me so many encouraging letters.

And, above all, thanks to the Author and Finisher of my faith, who was and is and is to come.

CHAPTER ONE

The Adventure Begins

"Do you think we're going to make it?" Christy Miller breathlessly asked her best friend, Katie, as the airport tram rumbled toward the terminal.

"We have to make it!" Katie said, looping her backpack over her shoulder. "The very second this tram comes to a stop, we're out of here. Grab your bag so we can be the first ones off."

Christy pulled her black shoulder bag off the luggage rack and moved closer to the tram door, right behind her determined, red-headed friend. "Do you remember which gate we're supposed to go to?"

"Fifty-four," Katie called over her shoulder just as they came to a bumpy stop. The dozen or so other passengers rose to their feet. "Come on!" Katie flew out the door with long-legged Christy right behind her. They trotted across the runway asphalt at San Francisco International Airport and took the terminal's steps two at a time.

"This is Gate 87," Christy said, scanning the signs above them as they entered the building.

"Which way to gate 54?" Katie loudly called out so anyone nearby could hear.

"At the end of this concourse turn left," a uniformed desk clerk responded. "Go past concourse E and keep going until you reach the International Central Terminal."

Christy was about to ask for clearer directions, but Katie was already hustling her way through the crowds. "Wait!" Christy yelled, and she hurried to catch up.

It was bad enough their flight from the Orange County airport had been delayed more than an hour. She didn't need to be separated from Katie and miss their flight to London.

"We only have twenty minutes!" Katie said as Christy fell into step with her. "Doug was right. We should have taken that earlier flight with Tracy. This is crazy!"

"I hope Doug made his flight up from San Diego okay," Christy puffed. Her hair was tangled in the shoulder strap of her black bag. She yanked it off her right shoulder, and a few long, nutmeg strands came with it. "Ouch!"

"Left here," Katie directed at the end of the concourse. She broke into a jog, her green backpack bobbing up and down as she athletically maneuvered her way through the crowds as if she were running an obstacle course. Christy fell in line behind her, keeping her eyes on the bobbing green backpack.

This is impossible. We're never going to make it. I can't believe I let Katie talk me into another one of her crazy adventures!

Katie stopped in front of an opening to another concourse. "Is this the international terminal?" she asked a man in a business suit.

He shrugged and kept walking. Katie approached another man stepping off the escalator.

"Keep going that way. All the way to the end."

"Thanks." Katie burst into a full run. All Christy could do was follow. She felt the perspiration bead up on her forehead and wished she hadn't worn so many layers.

They had been instructed by the missionary organization in England to dress warmly for this January outreach trip, but right now Christy wished she had packed her coat instead of worn it. Her shoulder bag felt as if it weighed a hundred pounds, and she wished she had taken Katie's advice and brought a backpack instead. What else had she miscalculated? Was this whole trip a mistake?

"Come on!" Katie yelled over her shoulder when she noticed that Christy had fallen behind.

With one last burst of adrenaline, Christy pushed herself to catch up with Katie, fully aware that in this whole throng of travelers, they were the only ones running.

"Doug!" Christy heard Katie yell. "Over here!"

Doug stood by the entrance of the international concourse, head and shoulders above the rest of the crowd. His usually boyish grin was replaced by a frown, which Christy had rarely seen in the few months they had been dating. She wanted to fall into his arms and feel one of his reassuring hugs, but there was no time.

"Quick!" Doug said. "Get in line for the metal detector. Over there. Hurry! Our plane leaves in five minutes!"

Katie and Christy immediately followed his instructions and passed through the archway, fortunately without setting off any alarms.

"Tickets, please," the woman behind the check-in counter said. She looked unruffled. The girls scrambled for their tickets and passports. The attendant tore off a portion of their tickets and said, "Gate 54. To the right. They've already boarded."

"Come on, you guys, let's go!" Doug's coach-like holler was a stark contrast to the ticket agent's relaxed attitude.

Christy realized that Tracy must be sitting alone on the plane, waiting for them. They *had* to make this flight. The three of them ran to the gate just as the door began to close.

"Wait!" Doug sprinted ahead. "We're on this flight."

The man held the door open with his foot as another attendant reached for their tickets and quickly scanned them. "You just made it."

Only a few more pounding paces, and they were on the plane.

"I can't believe this," Christy said under her breath. She handed the flight attendant her ticket stub.

"Your seat is in row 34. That's all the way in the back."

"Naturally," Katie muttered. Clutching her backpack in front of her, she led the way down the narrow airplane aisle.

Christy was the first to spot petite Tracy, planted in the middle of row 34. Her heart-shaped face had taken on a stern, defender-of-the-seats look.

"That was *not* funny, you guys," Tracy said, scrunching up her delicate nose and trying not to look mean or terrified or both. "I almost got off the plane! I decided if you guys didn't show up in two more minutes, I was going to get off the plane. No way was I going to fly to London by myself!"

"We made it. A bit on the close side, I'd say." Doug popped open the overhead compartment and stuffed Katie and Christy's bags in next to his and Tracy's.

"You'll need to take a seat, please, sir," the flight attendant said with a definite British accent.

Doug lowered himself into the aisle seat next to Christy. Katie, on the other side of her, began to fill Tracy and Doug in on their morning's delay. Christy closed her eyes and drew in a deep breath. She felt like crying. Or laughing. Or something. Then she felt Doug's strong hand covering hers.

"You okay?" he asked softly.

Christy opened her eyes and looked into Doug's gentle, understanding face. "That was too close," she said. She was still thinking, *This is too much. This is crazy. Why am I here?*

"We made it. We're on our way to England," Doug said, wiping the perspiration from his forehead with the back of his shirt sleeve. The boyish grin returned. "Can you believe this?"

"No," Christy whispered, feeling Doug's hand squeeze hers. "I can't. It all happened so fast."

"Yeah, but we made it," Doug pointed out as the flight attendants began their presentation on the aircraft's safety features. "I wish more people from the God Lovers' group could have come. I'm glad the four of us made it."

"Doug, four and a half weeks was not exactly a long time for everyone to raise support and get passports and everything," Christy said. "If we would have waited until the summer to do this outreach, I'm sure a lot more people could have come."

Doug shrugged his broad shoulders. "I figure if the four of us return with great reports of the trip, everyone will want to go this summer, and we can do it all over again."

"If we do, I'm definitely taking the early morning flight like Tracy did, even if it does mean getting up at five in the morning! You were right about that one." Christy pulled off her coat and fanned her red face with her hand.

Doug smiled. She could tell he liked being told he was right. Not in an arrogant way, but in a big brother, Doug way.

The plane was now taxiing down the runway, about to take off.

"Did the mission send you the final information?" Christy asked. "That's the only part my parents were concerned about. I gave them the address we'll be at the first two nights in London and the place we'll have our training. But I think they were concerned I didn't know where our outreach assignment would be for the last two weeks of the trip."

"All I received from the mission in the fax yesterday were directions on how to get to Carnforth Hall for the week of training. Don't worry," Doug said as the nose of the plane tilted up and they took off into the wild blue yonder. "God will direct our paths. These next three weeks will be an awesome chance for us to trust Him."

Christy had to smile. She had known Doug since she was fourteen. In those four and a half years, he had hardly changed. As a matter of fact, he was saying "awesome" the day she had met him. He had grown taller and more muscular, but still, he looked the same, acted the same, and even dressed about the same.

But in those years Christy had changed a lot. She had grown up. Now eighteen and a half and a college freshman, she felt as if she were almost the same age as Doug, a twenty-three-year-old with only eight credits to go before completing his bachelor's degree in business.

"Doug," Tracy asked, leaning past Katie and Christy, "did you receive a confirmation for the Bed and Breakfast we're supposed to stay at in London tonight?"

"Yep."

"And did you get the train tickets for us to Carnforth Hall?"

"We buy them at the airport. I have all the information."

"What about the schedule?" Katie asked. "When do we have to be at Carnforth?"

"Friday afternoon."

"Did you get that tour book of London?" Tracy asked. "There's so much to see. How are we going to get to it all in only two days?"

"Will you guys relax?" Doug said. "I've got it covered. Once they turn off the seat belt sign, I'll get my tour book down and we'll make some plans."

Christy felt as if all she had been doing for the past month was make plans. It still amazed her that her parents had agreed to let her spend her semester break with her three closest friends on the other side of the world.

It was even more amazing that Katie's parents had agreed. They had never been in favor of her taking off on trips with the church youth group. But they saw it more as a cultural experience than a missions trip. Tracy and Doug were both older than Katie and Christy, and they both came from very supportive families. Christy's parents were supportive, of course, although they tended to be a little more on the protective side.

Her dad's final words last night had been, "I hope this trip helps you figure out what you want to do with your life. You know your mother and I will support you, whatever you decide. But you need to know it's time for you to decide."

At the time she had bristled at his words. Making decisions had never been her strong point. Christy had made plenty of decisions she had regretted later. The biggest one had to be last spring when she broke up with Todd, Doug's best friend. Todd had a once-in-a-lifetime opportunity before him, and Christy didn't want to hold him back. At the time, she knew it was the right thing to do, but it had taken her months to recover from the loss.

It had taken Doug even longer to convince Christy that she should go out with him. She had wavered in her decision all summer, and it was October before she finally agreed to be Doug's girlfriend.

The funny part was, nothing much had changed between

them during the three months they had been going together. They were close friends, but they always had been. He held her hand more, but he never kissed her. It was a comfortable, secure friendship, and one her parents felt good enough about to let their daughter fly to Europe with Doug.

Doug clicked open his seat belt, stood, and reached for the tour books in his backpack. For the next hour, the four of them made big plans about all they would see in London. To Christy, it still seemed like a dream.

Dinner was served—sliced beef with gravy, peas, fruit salad, and a piece of spice cake with chopped nuts, which she gave to Doug. Nuts had never been Christy's favorite. Tea was served with milk and sugar, and Christy sipped at the steaming brew, feeling grown-up and important. Maybe she could do this international thing after all.

As soon as their tray tables were cleared, the movie began. Christy couldn't see over the head of the guy in front of her, so she gave up on the movie and asked Doug to hand her bag to her from the overhead bin. She found her journal and began to write.

The adventure begins! I'm on the plane now, between Doug and Katie, and we are actually flying to England. I still can't believe this. I feel as if everything in my life has been rushing past me these last few months, and I'm caught up in the current.

My dad was right in urging me to make some decisions about the future. I don't know what I want to be. I don't know if I like being grown-up. And when did that happen, anyhow? I must be grown-up if I'm on my way to England. I can't believe I'm in college. Sometimes I feel so independent, and other times I wish I could go back to the simpler days when I would spend the whole day lying on the beach, doing nothing but watch Todd surf. Oops. I did it again; I mentioned the "T" word. I wasn't going to do that anymore. I know that . . .

"The 'T' word?" Katie asked, looking at the page.

Christy snapped her diary shut. "I thought you were watching the movie," she whispered harshly. She glanced at Doug. He had on his headset and seemed caught up in the action on the small screen in front of them.

"I can't believe you still even think about the 'T' word!" Katie whispered back. "It's been months—almost a year—since he left. The guy is gone. Long gone. Ancient history. You have absolutely no contact with him. He's most likely on some mosquito-infested tropical island serving God and loving it. If he still wanted you in his life, he would have written you. But then he's never written to you, has he, Christy? Ever. In your whole life. Think about it."

"Have you forgotten about the coconut he sent me from Hawaii?"

"Christy," Katie's piercing green eyes looked serious, "I couldn't tell you this if I weren't your best friend."

Christy looked away. She already knew what Katie was going to say. They had had this same conversation at the end of the summer when Katie tried to convince her to let go of Todd's memory and give Doug a fair chance.

"I know," Christy whispered, a tiny tear blurring her vision.

"No, I don't think you know, Chris. Otherwise we wouldn't be having this conversation." Katie sounded stern.

"Can we have it another time, Katie?" Christy said, blinking her blue-green eyes. "What I write in my diary is my business, not yours. You don't know what I'm thinking."

"I can make a pretty good guess."

"So what? I don't remember inviting you into my thoughts!" The instant Christy made the remark, she regretted it. This was not a good way to start off a three-week trip in which she and Katie would be together day and night. Especially when, in her heart, she knew Katie was right. She knew that part of her growing up and making decisions about her future had been hindered because she couldn't seem to get over Todd.

"Fine." Katie planted her headphones back over her ears and fixed her attention on the screen.

Christy reached over and squeezed Katie's arm to get her attention. Katie slowly turned to face Christy and lifted the headset off one ear.

"I'm sorry," Christy said.

"Don't worry about it. We'll talk later." Katie flashed a smile, squeezed Christy's arm back, and returned her attention to the movie.

Christy knew all was forgiven. She also knew Katie would make sure they talked later.

Glancing over at Doug, Christy wondered if he had heard any of their conversation. He had always been so patient and understanding with her.

The ultimate proof had been when Christy found out he had bought back her gold ID bracelet from a jewelry store two years ago. Todd had given her the bracelet. Then a sort-of-boyfriend, Rick, had stolen it from Christy and hocked it at a jewelry store so he could use the money to buy her a clunky silver one that said "Rick."

Her relationship with Rick had quickly dissolved, and she had begun to make payments to buy back the gold bracelet. Then one day the jeweler gave it to her, saying some guy had come in and paid for it in full.

It wasn't until last spring that Christy had found out Doug was the one who paid for it. He did it simply out of his love for Christy. It didn't matter to Doug that the bracelet was given to Christy by another guy, another guy who just happened to be his best friend and who had captured Christy's interest from the day she had first met them on the beach at Newport. During the years of friendship that followed for the three of them, Doug always took a backseat to Todd.

Anyone who knew them would be quick to say that Doug had waited patiently for Christy. He had never let his deep feelings for her come out until after she had broken up with Todd and had given the bracelet back to him. Not until Todd was on a plane headed for parts unknown did Doug let his feelings for Christy be known. Even then, he took it slow.

He had to be the most patient guy on the face of the earth. And, as Katie had pointed out last summer, since 1 Corinthians 13 described love as being patient, kind, not jealous, and always looking out for the best interest of others, then Doug must deeply love Christy.

Christy looped her arm through Doug's, which was balanced on the armrest between them, and leaned her head against his shoulder. Doug was a treasure. A treasure she should not take for granted. She knew girls who would do anything to have even a fraction of Doug's attention. And here she had it all. She knew she should appreciate him more.

Doug adjusted his position to make Christy more comfortable. She closed her eyes and told herself again that she was really, truly on an airplane on her way to London with the most wonderful—no, make that the most awesome—guy in the whole world and with her two best friends, Katie and Tracy. This trip would change her life forever. She had no doubt.

She vowed that nothing would ruin this trip for her or for her friends, especially not the memory of an invisible Todd.

CHAPTER TWO

Big Ben and Other Famous Stuff

"Do you think I exchanged enough money?" Katie asked, adjusting the shoulder straps on her backpack.

The four friends stood on the platform with their luggage gathered around their feet. They were waiting for the next underground train to arrive.

"I don't know," Katie continued. "A hundred dollars doesn't look like much when it's turned into pounds. And their money is so weird-looking! It looks like play money."

"Katie," Tracy said softly, leaning closer and making sure the crowd of local people standing around them couldn't hear, "I think it's obvious enough we're tourists without our announcing to all these people how much money we have on us and that we think their money looks weird."

Katie's straight red hair swished as she glanced around, checking out the audience Tracy seemed so concerned about. Quickly changing the subject and lowering her voice just a smidgen, Katie asked, "Are you sure we know which train to take?"

Doug patted the folded map in the pocket of his jacket. "I got us this far, didn't I? I think I can find the hotel. Did you guys keep your tube passes handy? We'll need to run them through the machine again when we leave the station."

"This reminds me of the BART trains in San Francisco," Tracy said softly. "Except those are above ground. Have you guys ever been on BART?"

None of them had.

"This system is slightly older," Doug said. "Did you see in that one tour book that they used to run steam engine trains down here more than a hundred years ago?"

Christy looked up at the rounded ceiling and then at the many large billboard posters scattered across the brick walls of the underground tunnel. She couldn't imagine people and trains being in this same tunnel a hundred years ago.

"Isn't it freaky, you guys," said Katie, "to think that there's a city above us? I don't feel like we're in London yet. Maybe I will when I see one of those red double-decker buses."

Just then a loud rush of air sounded through the dark passageway. A moment later the underground train came to a halt. Before Christy had time to situate her suitcase so she could wheel it onto the train, people began to push toward the open door. Her luggage, with a pop-up handle and wheels, had been a present from her wealthy Aunt Marti.

"Can you get it?" Doug asked as he noticed her struggling.

"Yes, I have it now." Christy pushed her suitcase toward the door, feeling Doug right behind her, prodding her onto the train.

Tracy found a seat inside and plopped down her bag, motioning for Christy or Doug to sit next to her. Katie was behind Doug. Christy sat next to Tracy and didn't notice the doors closing until she heard Katie's loud yelp. They looked up. All they could see was Katie's backside wedged between the two closing doors, keeping it open.

"You guys, help!" Katie yelled.

Christy wanted to burst out laughing but swallowed hard and hurried to help Doug pry open the door. They separated it far enough for Doug to yank Katie and her luggage inside the train just before it started to move.

"Katie, are you okay?" Tracy said. "You could have been killed! What were you thinking?"

"I was thinking I didn't want to get separated from you guys. That seems to be the theme of this trip, doesn't it?" Katie dropped her canvas suitcase on the floor at Christy's feet and held onto a long metal bar next to the seat. "I think we need to make a plan B here, Doug. If I hadn't made it on this train, I would have been completely lost. I don't even know where we're staying! How would I ever have found you guys? We need a little more teamwork."

"You're right," Doug said, reaching for the back of Christy's seat to steady himself as the train picked up speed and jostled them from side to side. The four of them huddled closer together, Christy and Tracy in the seats and Katie and Doug standing above them. Christy felt sure they were a humorous spectacle to all the other passengers.

"Okay," Doug said, assuming his coach voice, "we're staying at the Miles Hampton on Seymore Street. We get off at Hyde Park. It's only a few blocks' walk to the hotel. If you guys need help with your luggage, just tell me. And let's make an agreement that we'll all stick together and look out for each other, okay?"

Doug's "few blocks" turned into more like a few miles. Either that, or they were lost.

"Can I look at the map again?" Katie asked, stopping in front of another row of houses that looked just like the row of houses on the last street they had walked up. "Are you sure this place is a hotel?"

"It's a Bed and Breakfast," Doug said, willingly dropping the canvas luggage he held in both hands and reaching for the map. "My parents stayed there a couple of years ago. They said it was easy to find. Look, here's Seymore Street. What street are we on now?"

Christy parked her rolling suitcase and gladly took the heavy black bag off her shoulder. She couldn't believe how tired she was from walking. For the first time since they began their parade through the streets of London, Christy stopped and drew in the sights around her. Tall, narrow brick houses lined the street. Black taxis drove past them on the "wrong" side of the road. Noisy cars and buses honked their horns. A small, furry dog at the end of his owner's leash barked at them as they walked past. From across the street came the merry sound of a little bell clinking as a woman entered a bakery.

"Uh-oh," Christy said, looking up into the thick, gray sky and lifting her open palm heavenward. "I hope we're almost there because it's starting to rain."

That's when she noticed how cold it was. They had been walking so hard and so fast, she hadn't realized the damp cold was creeping up her legs. Her jeans weren't protection enough against the bitter cold, and her legs began to feel prickly and chilled to the bone.

"This way," Doug said, heading down the street with long, deliberate strides. "Only two more blocks."

This time he was right. And it was a good thing. Just as they huddled under the bright blue canopy over the Miles Hampton door, the mist that had been teasing them for the past two blocks turned into a respectable London downpour.

The door was locked, so Katie rang the door buzzer a couple of times. A rosy-cheeked, white-haired woman peeked at them through the lace curtains drawn across the window in the door. "Who's the impatient one?" she said brightly as she opened the door. "Come in, come in! It won't do to have you catching cold your first day."

It took only a few minutes to check in at the quaint "B and B," as the woman called the Bed and Breakfast. Then they lugged their suitcases up four winding flights of stairs to the top floor, where two rooms awaited them. The girls' room had three twin beds and a separate bathroom with the biggest bathtub Christy had ever seen. The house was old, but it had been nicely restored; the room was clean and fresh. Christy noticed how puffy the flowered bedspreads looked, and she flopped down on the nearest bed.

Tracy did the same, face first on the bed next to Christy. "This pillow is calling my name," Tracy said. "It wants me to stay right here with it all day."

Christy heard the rain tap dancing on their window. She couldn't help but agree with Tracy. After all, it was three in the morning back home; none of them had slept on the plane during the ten-hour flight. A little nap would feel so good.

"Ready, gang?" Katie called, bursting through the door with Doug right behind her. "Let's go see London."

Christy and Tracy groaned.

"You guys definitely got the better of the two rooms," Doug said, surveying their wallpapered surroundings. "My room isn't bad. It just feels more like I'm sleeping in an attic. Slanted ceiling. Kind of squishy. You even have a bathroom."

"You don't?"

"I get to use the one at the end of the hall on the floor below us," Doug said. "I don't mind, really. For the money, this is a great place. Besides, we're not going to hang around here. We've got a city to explore!"

"Doug's right, you guys," Katie said, stepping into the bathroom and running some water in the sink to wash her face. "The worst thing we could do would be to sleep now. We have to stay up all day to trick our internal clocks into thinking it's daytime now and not nighttime. Hey, how do you get warm water out of this thing?"

Doug joined her in the bathroom and demonstrated how to use the sink stopper to fill the sink with hot and cold water at the same time, resulting in warm water.

"You mean only hot water comes out of this side and only cold out of this side? How archaic!"

"I hate to break this to you, Toto, but we're not in Kansas anymore," Doug said, sticking his fingers in the water and sprinkling Katie's face. "This is a very old city. This is a very old house. It would follow that the plumbing would be a little on the archaic side."

Doug dipped his fingers in the sink again and took three steps over to Christy's bed where he sprinkled her. "Wake up! It's time to have some fun."

"Tracy," Christy said, "I think the ceiling is leaking. I feel a drip."

"Yeah, I hear a drip," Tracy agreed.

"Oh, yeah?" Doug said. Before Christy or Tracy realized what was happening, Doug had dunked a hand towel into the full sink and began to wring it out over Tracy's head. She screamed, jumped up, and started to laugh. "Doug! We're not at the beach! You can't go around splashing girls with water in London. It isn't proper!"

They all laughed at Tracy's fake British accent, which she

attempted to employ on the last two sentences.

"Besides, Doug, it's raining out there, and it's so cozy in here," Christy said in a pretend whine.

"I can make it rain inside too!" Doug threatened Christy with his wet hand towel.

"Okay, okay. Let me brush my hair first." Christy traded places with Katie in the bathroom and closed the door behind her. Her reflection in the mirror startled her. Her cheeks were red, and her brown hair lay flat against her head, hanging lifelessly a few inches past her shoulders.

She thought of how cute Tracy's short hair looked. She had cut it short, just below her ears, especially for this trip. Tracy's hair had a lot of natural body and had kept its shape with only a quick brushing when they had landed at Heathrow Airport.

Christy wondered if she should have gotten her hair cut short for the trip too. She knew Doug liked it long. She liked it long. It just looked so blah.

After trying to pull it back with a headband, put it in a ponytail, and quickly braid it, she gave up.

"Are you still alive in there?" Katie asked, knocking on the door.

"My hair is driving me crazy!" Christy said.

"You're going to drive us crazy!" Katie yelled.

"Okay, okay." Christy shook out her mane, washed her face, and stuck a scrunchie in her pocket in case she wanted to try a ponytail later. She opened the bathroom door, ready to go. A bright light flashed in her face.

"Thanks, Christy," Katie said. "You've become my first official photo in London. Let's go see what other funny-looking stuff we can take pictures of."

"Oh, thanks a lot," Christy said, reaching for her coat and

following her friends down the long, winding stairs and into the front lobby.

"I want to get a close-up shot of one of those guards who stands in one place all day and never flinches," Katie said. "Maybe I can get him to give me a little smile."

"Food first," Doug said as they stepped outside, all bundled up and holding their umbrellas high. "We must keep our priorities straight."

The first food they found was, of all things, a Kentucky Fried Chicken restaurant.

"I didn't come all the way to England to eat Kentucky Fried Chicken," Katie said, looking down the street for signs of any other kind of restaurant.

"Come on," Tracy pleaded. "It's only a snack. We'll find some fun English place for lunch. I don't think Doug can hold out much longer."

"Thanks, Trace," Doug said, collapsing his umbrella and stepping inside the all-too-familiar-looking fast-food restaurant.

They all ordered from a lit-up menu above the counter that looked just like one from home. The only difference was the currency.

"That's one pound, forty-five 'P,' miss," the man behind the counter told Christy. Christy handed him a ten-pound note and received a handful of change and a five-pound note. She joined the others at a table by the window.

"Isn't this money weird?" Katie said, examining her change.

"Katie," Tracy said, "didn't we already go over the weird money thing?"

Christy was aware that the elderly couple at the table next to them was watching. She was also aware of how quiet it was for a restaurant full of people. Everyone else seemed to be speaking softly and keeping to themselves.

In comparison, Katie was extraordinarily loud. It bothered Christy. She guessed it was bothering Tracy too. Doug seemed unaffected.

He pulled out his handy-dandy map and pocket-size tour book and stated, "Okay, so we'll see Big Ben first, then the crown jewels at the Tower of London. We take bus 16, I think. No, maybe it's bus 11."

"Let me see that," Katie said, snatching the tour book away from Doug. "Oh, Charles Dickens' house. That would be an interesting tour. Let's go there after the Tower of London."

"It's on the opposite side of town, Katie," Doug said.

"No, it's not. Look, it's right here by . . . oh, you're right. Okay, then let's go to St. Paul's Cathedral. That's only two inches away from the Tower of London."

"Let's just go and see what we can see," Tracy suggested, tossing her trash into a bin that was marked "rubbish."

Christy was glad it wasn't up to her to plot their course or decipher how to get there. She was happy being a follower and letting Katie and Doug be the pioneers.

They hopped on a bus near the Marble Arch that took them to Piccadilly Circus. Doug told them to get off and look for bus 12, which would take them to Parliament and Big Ben.

Riding on the top of the double-decker bus was fun, Christy thought, because she had a good view of the bustling streets below and of the statues and monuments everywhere. What she didn't like was getting off, shivering under her umbrella, and listening to Doug and Katie argue. She also hated feeling lost and confused.

It seemed worse when they got off in front of the huge, architecturally intricate Parliament Building and found that the famous old clock, Big Ben, was so shrouded in fog that it hardly seemed worth the effort to take a picture. Christy did, however. Her camera, a gift last year from Uncle Bob, had served her well during her senior year as a photographer on the yearbook staff. She knew when she returned home she would be glad she had the pictures, even if they were all gray and foggy.

"Well, that was a thrill," Katie said, spinning around and blocking Christy's viewfinder with her umbrella. "What's next?"

Without saying anything to Katie, Christy took a few steps to the right and adjusted her zoom again before snapping a picture of Big Ben. "Why don't you guys all stand there by the fence, and I'll take a picture of you with Parliament in the background?"

The three obliged, umbrellas bumping each other and people passing in front of the camera. Christy snapped the picture, then turned around and snapped a shot of the street behind them with a black taxi and a red bus passing each other in the heavy traffic.

"Do you want to see the River Thames?" Doug asked. "According to this map, it's right over there, beyond that park."

"What's to see?" Katie asked.

"It's a famous river," Doug said. "Come on. Have a little adventure, Katie."

"I *did* have a little adventure. I saw Big Ben. Now I want a *big* adventure. I want to see the jewels and the guards in the big furry hats."

"We're so close to the river," Tracy said. "Maybe we should look at it so we can at least say we saw it."

"Whatever we do, could we take a bus?" Christy asked. "My legs are freezing!" She wished she had taken the time to put on a pair of tights when they were at the hotel. She felt cold. Wet cold. Miserable cold.

"It's only a quick walk to the river," Doug said, taking

Christy's hand. "If we walk fast, you'll warm up. Come on."

Off they went to the river. In Katie's words, the wide, gray, fog-mantled water looked "like Big Ben, only horizontal and without numbers."

They were hoofing it back to catch another bus when Tracy noticed an old, interesting-looking building on their left.

"Let's check the tour book, Doug. I'm sure that's something important," Tracy said.

Christy hated standing still in the drizzle. She stomped her feet to get them warm and to shake the chill off her legs. "You guys," Tracy exclaimed, "that's Westminster Abbey!"

"Great," said Katie. "What's that?"

"It's a very old church," Tracy said, scanning the tour book. "It says here this site was first used as a place of worship in the year A.D. 604. Can you even imagine how old that is? And listen to this: 'Since the eleventh century, the church has been the coronation site of English kings and queens.' We have to see it, you guys. There's a bunch of famous people buried there. Charles Dickens is buried there!"

Katie noticed that the drizzle had let up and closed her umbrella while Tracy was reading. With squinting eyes she moved in for a closer look at Tracy. "Are you serious here, girl? You really want to go look at a bunch of old dead people?"

"This is Westminster Abbey. It's famous, Katie!"

"Well, so was Big Ben. And that turned out to be a real dud!"

"Can I cut in here, you two?" Doug said, closing his umbrella and stepping in between them. "I think we're all pretty tired and hungry. Why don't we find someplace to eat and decide what to do next after we've had some food."

"Great idea," Christy said. "I'm freezing. I think my socks got wet. My feet are numb."

"What do you say, ladies? A nice spot of tea, perhaps?"

They couldn't help but release their tension when they heard Doug try a British accent on his last sentence. Then following their trail back up the road toward Trafalgar Square, the four cold, wet, weary travelers went in search of a quiet little restaurant and a hot cup of tea.

CHAPTER THREE

A Cup of Tea

"No wonder the English like tea so much," Christy said, holding a white china cup with both hands. She sipped her tea as if it were warming her to her toes. "If I lived here, I'd be looking for something to warm me up several times a day too."

Katie took her last bite of fish and said, "The vinegar was okay on this fish, but I still like good old American tartar sauce. You want the rest of my fries, Doug?"

"Sure, I'll take your chips," he said, using the British word for fries.

"I have a question," Tracy said. "If they call french fries 'chips,' then what do they call potato chips?"

" 'Crisps,' " their waiter said, reaching to clear Katie's empty plate.

They had stumbled into a quaint-looking restaurant and found a table with four chairs as if it were waiting for them. The waiter had turned out to be friendly. The four orders of fish and chips had come in huge portions with the mushiest green peas Christy had ever seen. She ate about half her fried fish, half her chips, and only a reluctant spoonful of the mushy peas. They tasted the same as they looked.

Doug managed to put away whatever food the girls left, including the peas. Christy decided he must have been born without taste buds. Either that or his bottomless stomach was so demanding it left little room for a discerning palate.

Doug stuck the last few cold chips in his mouth and glanced at his watch. "It's a little after four. What do you think? Should we try to make it to the Tower of London to see the jewels now, or wait until tomorrow?"

"We would have more time tomorrow," Tracy suggested.

"Where did this day go?" Christy asked. "And what day is it, anyhow?"

"Wednesday," Doug said. "It's eight in the morning at home right now. Time to start today."

"Isn't that weird?" Katie said. "At home everyone is just starting this day, and we're almost done with it."

Once again Christy could see Tracy cringing at Katie's loud voice and her declaration of something else that was weird. It bugged Christy, too, but not as much as it seemed to irk Tracy.

"So what do you guys want to do? It'll be dark soon," Doug said.

"Let's see as much as we can," Tracy said. "Even if it's dark. We only have today and tomorrow. We've come all this way and there's so much to see. Would you guys be willing to go back to Westminster Abbey? I'd really like to see it."

"Sure," Doug answered for all of them. "Let's figure out this bill and get out of here."

Christy noticed as they walked briskly down the street toward the ancient Gothic church that Katie was unusually quiet. Tension between Katie and Tracy seemed to be growing, and Christy felt uneasy about it.

Over the years, Doug and Katie had experienced plenty of

friendly conflicts, but through all their tumbles, their friendship always managed to land on its feet. Katie and Doug had a brother-sister kind of esteem for each other.

Tracy and Doug had been close friends even longer than Christy and Tracy. As a matter of fact, Doug and Tracy even dated for a while several years ago. The two of them had remained close friends, and Christy couldn't remember ever hearing either of them saying anything unkind about the other. They seemed to get along in any kind of situation.

But Katie and Tracy had never spent an extended amount of time together. Their personalities were so different, yet so alike. They were both strong, determined women: Katie in an outward, aggressive manner, and Tracy in her gentle, firm, uncompromising way.

Then, as if Tracy sensed the same tension with Katie, she fell back a few steps next to Katie, and Christy heard her say, "I really appreciate you being flexible. I'm looking forward to going to the Tower of London tomorrow. We'll have more time then. I'm sure it'll work out and be much better than trying to go now."

Katie didn't respond at first. Then, as they crossed the street to Westminster Abbey, Christy heard Katie say, "Do you always get your way, Tracy?"

Christy wanted to turn around and scold Katie for saying such a thing, but Doug quickly looped his arm around Christy's shoulders and spoke softly in her ear. "Let the two of them work it out, Chris. Trust me. It's the best way for both of them."

Christy had to trust Doug. There wasn't much she could do. She strained to listen as Tracy, in her gentle yet firm way, told Katie they needed to work together as a team and do what was best for the group.

"Right," Katie responded. "It would help, though, if the

group were making more of the decisions and not just you."

"You're right, Katie. After this, we'll all decide what to do next," Tracy said.

They were at the door of the old stone building, and Christy realized she had hardly paid attention to what the church looked like. She entered solemnly. A sign by the door indicated an admission fee of three pounds.

"Three pounds!" Katie blurted out. "I'm not paying to go inside a church! I'm waiting right here. You guys can go in without me."

"I think the charge is only for a tour, Katie," Doug said quietly. "I don't think we have to pay anything to look around this part."

The four entered the tourist-filled sanctuary with Katie lagging behind. They walked around, quietly observing the statues, memorials, and engravings on the stone floor that identified who was buried beneath their feet.

"Look," Doug said to Christy, pointing to the large letters etched on the floor in front of him. "David Livingstone is buried here. He was that famous missionary to Africa. Did you know that they brought his body back here to England, but they took out his heart and buried it in Africa because that's where his heart was—with the African people? Is that awesome or what?"

Christy wasn't sure it was awesome. *Bizarre* might be a better adjective. It sounded like something Todd would do.

Todd. Where did that thought come from?

Christy impulsively reached over, took Doug's hand, and squeezed it tight. "Doug, do you want to be a missionary to some far-off place?"

"You mean like Todd?"

Is he reading my thoughts? Or is he thinking the same things about Todd that I am?

"I don't know," Doug said thoughtfully, looking down at the floor once more. "That's why I wanted to come on this outreach. To see if I have what it takes. I'm not like Todd."

"I know," Christy said quickly. "And I don't want you to be. I want you to be Doug. And you are . . ." Now her thoughts seemed scrambled, and she felt angry that she hadn't been able to leave thoughts of Todd back on the airplane. Back in California. Back in her collection of high school memories. Todd had followed both of them to England and once again stood between them. ". . . I just wondered if you had thought much about being a missionary." Christy held Doug's hand tighter. She wanted to think of Doug and only Doug.

"Not really. With my business major I've pictured myself being in the American workforce at some big company and sort of being a missionary to all the lost business people. I don't think I could live overseas."

"Me either," Tracy whispered. Christy hadn't noticed her standing on the other side of Doug. "I mean, this is fun to visit, but I do better in familiar surroundings. What about you, Christy?"

"I don't know. That's why I wanted to come on this trip too. I don't know what I want to do with my life. Or, I guess I should say, I don't know what God wants to do with my life." Saying it aloud sounded even scarier than when she had thought it or written it in her diary. It was like admitting she was lost, aimlessly taking general ed. courses at a junior college and trying to come up with answers for the career counselors who asked what she was interested in. She honestly didn't know.

A uniformed gentleman politely asked if they would like to

take a seat because it was time for evening vespers to begin. Katie was already sitting in one of the folding chairs set up in the section where they were standing. The three of them joined her, with Doug taking the initiative and sitting next to Katie.

Within a few minutes a line of choir boys wearing white and red robes with high white lace collars flowed down the center aisle, two by two. They stepped right over the David Livingstone engraved stone on their way to the altar at the front of the chapel.

Christy closed her eyes and breathed in the majesty of the moment as the clear, high voices of the choir danced off the rounded stone ceiling of this ancient place of worship. During the music and Bible reading that followed, Christy quietly bowed her head and worshiped the same awesome God whom people had sought to worship on this site for more than a thousand years. The thought sobered her and made her feel a reverence she had never felt in her church at home in California.

She tried to explain it to her friends the next morning as they ate breakfast together in the small dining room of their Bed and Breakfast. Christy sat with her back to a huge fireplace where a cheery fire crackled and warmed her. Doug seemed to know what she was saying, and Tracy agreed between bites of crisp toast. Katie ate silently, studying a tour book and not entering into the conversation.

Things had not been good between Katie and Tracy that morning. Katie had washed her hair and had asked to borrow Tracy's hair dryer.

"Be sure to plug in the adapter first," Tracy said.

Katie had plugged the adapter into one electric outlet and the hair dryer into another. When she turned on the hair dryer, it sounded like a lawn mower. In less than ten seconds the dryer started to spit sparks into their room. Then, with a loud pop,

Tracy's hair dryer had burned out.

Tracy's face had turned deep red as she followed the cord from her dead hair dryer to the outlet and said, "Katie, you're supposed to plug the hair dryer *into* the adapter!"

"How was I supposed to know? All you said was to plug in the adapter first, and I did!"

Tracy grabbed her awful-smelling dryer from Katie's hand, threw it in the trash can, and said in a controlled voice, "That's okay. Don't worry about it."

At the time Christy had thought it would have been better if Tracy had hauled off and slugged Katie. Katie could have taken that. Instead, the two of them hadn't spoken one word to each other since.

"You want the rest of your eggs and sausages?" Doug asked Christy, eyeing her half-full breakfast plate.

"No. Go ahead, help yourself." Reaching for the silver teapot in the center of their table, Christy poured herself another cup of hot tea, tempering it quickly with milk and sugar.

"Would anyone else like some tea?" Christy asked.

"No, thanks," Katie said without looking up from the tour book.

"Which bus do we take to the Tower of London?" Doug asked.

"There's a bunch that will take us there once we get on Oxford Street. Do you remember how to get back to Oxford Street?"

Doug thought he knew, and within a half-hour they were bundled, umbrellaed, and armed with their cameras. Christy wore tights and leggings under her jeans today, and two pairs of socks. She could feel the difference when they hit the pavement and marched to Oxford Street in the foggy drizzle. Much warmer.

Today, more than the day before, she felt as if she were in England. And she liked it.

She enjoyed her top-deck perch again on the bus as they slowly edged their way down crowded Oxford Street. It seemed quite a while later when Doug asked Katie for the map and said, "Did that street say 'Bloomsbury'? We're going the wrong way."

"No, we're not," Katie said. "This is bus 8. Bus 8 goes to here," she said, leaning over and pointing to the map. "Then we switch to number 25, and it takes us right there."

"Yeah, but look," Doug said, pointing to the map. "This is the street we just passed. The Tower of London is way down here. We went the wrong way. This where we are now. Way up here."

"I don't believe this!" Katie said.

"Wait," Doug said. "Look here. We're not far from Charles Dickens' house. You wanted to go there, didn't you? We could take a quick tour and then catch bus 25."

"That's a great idea," Tracy said. "I'd love to see Dickens' home."

It turned out to be a good idea, even though they got lost and walked block after block, trying to find 48 Doughty Street, which wasn't well marked. Katie complained when they discovered the admission charge was two pounds. They took off in separate directions to explore the home of this author who had made old England come alive in his *A Christmas Carol, Oliver Twist, Great Expectations*, and dozens of other works.

Christy thought it was pretty interesting, especially the flimsy-looking quill pen displayed under glass that Dickens used to write his stories. She couldn't imagine what it would be like to write with a feather pen. Especially an entire book. Dozens of books. Writing back then must have been hard work.

Tracy and Doug seemed absorbed in all the displays, lingering to read the information cards much longer than Christy had the patience for. She left the two of them on the third floor, examining a huge painting of a lighthouse, and went down the narrow winding stairs in search of Katie. She found her sitting on a small wooden bench near the front door.

"Are you ready to go?" Christy asked.

Katie didn't look up as Christy sat next to her but waited for a group of tourists to meander down to the basement before answering, "Why am I being such a brat?"

"We're all kind of tired, Katie."

"I know, but that shouldn't be an excuse. I like Tracy. I really do. It's just that she's . . . I don't know. She gets to me."

"I think it's because you two are so much alike."

"No, we're not!"

"You each show it differently, but you're both strong and zealous. That's not a bad thing. I think it's a great quality."

Katie seemed thoughtful. She let out a deep breath. "Things somehow aren't the way I thought they would be."

"How did you think it would be?"

"Exciting and interesting and, well . . . much more fun than this. This is a lot of walking, getting lost, being frustrated, and feeling weird. I feel out of place. I'm not into all this ancient museum stuff. And it makes me feel uncultured and ignorant. I'm on new-experience sensory overload. I've never heard of any of these people we've seen statues of. And when Doug was explaining that stuff about the battles and statues at Trafalgar or whatever that square was, he might as well have been talking about life on another planet. I hate being so clueless about everything!"

Christy had always appreciated Katie's honesty and her ability to express her feelings accurately. "I know what you're saying," Christy said, trying to sound as comforting as possible.

"Then why doesn't it bother you? When I saw you holding your little cup of tea at breakfast, you looked as if you belonged here. As if it all came naturally to you. How do you do that?"

"I don't know. I guess it hasn't hit me yet. I like experiencing all these new things."

Just then Doug and Tracy came thumping down the stairs, talking intensely about a photograph they had seen of Hans Christian Andersen when he had come from Denmark to visit Dickens, whose work he admired. They kept their discussion going even after the four of them left and headed back to catch the bus. At least *they* were getting along well.

Katie seemed a little less tense as they boarded the bus and headed for the Tower of London. Christy should have know that Katie would be more relaxed once she had blown off a little steam.

As the bus lurched to a stop at an intersection, Christy caught a glimpse of her reflection in the window. She looked different. Scholarly maybe, with her hair back in a braid, almost no makeup on and wearing a turtleneck. All she needed was a pair of wire-rimmed glasses. It occurred to her that she looked like a person who knew where she was going in life. The thought made her smile. At least she could look the part. And before this trip was over, maybe she would feel the part too.

As she stomped her feet to warm them up, Christy thought how nice a hot cup of tea would taste right now.

CHAPTER FOUR

Carnforth Hall

"Where did our sunshine go?" Christy asked, peering out the window of the train as it sped out of London to the north.

An hour earlier they had made their way, luggage and all, to the Euston train station. Their backs had been teased by a brief stream of welcome sunbeams. But now the sky had pulled up its thick, gray winter blanket and tucked the sun back into bed.

When none of her friends answered her question, Christy switched her attention to the seats and found everyone else was asleep. Doug, sitting next to her, slept with his head tilted back and his mouth half-opened. He looked as if he might start to snore any minute. Christy wondered if she should wake him if he did.

Katie and Tracy, seated across the table and facing Doug and Christy, had each found her own space: Tracy with her head resting on a wadded-up sweater against the cold glass window and Katie, opposite Doug, with her head buried in her folded arms on top of the table.

Christy wasn't sure why she was still awake. It had been a strenuous early morning romp to get to the train on time. Now the train's constant sway and roll should have been enough to lull

35

anyone to sleep, especially someone who had gotten so little rest in the past three days.

But Christy was too excited. This was England! She didn't want to close her eyes and miss anything. The view outside her window changed from city sights, with red brick homes and black wrought-iron fences, to country sights with long stretches of meadow broken by neatly trimmed hedgerows. The bushes were all brown and naked, awaiting the kiss of spring to grace them with a fresh new wardrobe. And the fields looked almost a silver-gray color, with only a hint of the rich green grass that hid beneath the unbroken frost now covering the land.

I've got to write about this, Christy thought, searching in her bag for her journal. She remembered Charles Dickens' quill pen as she clicked the top of her ballpoint pen. She was glad she didn't have to try to write with quill and ink on this moving train table.

We're on a train on our way to Lancashire, which is somewhere in northwest England, she wrote. *Everyone is asleep but me. I love the countryside, even though it's all shrouded with a winter frost. I'm warm and cozy inside this comfortable train. If we make our connection in Manchester, we should arrive at Carnforth Hall before dinner and in time for the opening meeting of our outreach training.*

How can I describe London? What a huge, ancient, modern, bustling, polite, quaint, crowded, exhausting city! Two days were not enough to make its acquaintance. We did finally see the crown jewels at the Tower of London, like Katie wanted, and it was pretty interesting. But my favorite part was climbing to the top of St. Paul's Cathedral and looking down on the city. St. Paul's is such an incredible church. I've never been inside a huge church like that before, and it made me feel full of reverence and awe.

Doug stirred in his sleep and adjusted his large frame so that his left leg stuck out in the aisle and his head bobbed over toward Christy.

"You can lean on my shoulder if you want," she whispered. He must have been too far gone to hear her, because he didn't respond. Christy continued in her diary.

I also liked the words that were etched in the stone at the front of one of the churches. I think it was Westminster Abbey. Christy had copied them onto a scrap of paper and now dug for it in her bag.

"May God grant to the living, grace; to the departed, rest; to the church and the world, peace and concord; and to us sinners, eternal life."

Christy wasn't sure why this inscription intrigued her so much, except for the way it focused on grace and peace and "concord," or harmony. Those were not exactly qualities their foursome had experienced so far on this trip. She hoped that would change once their training began at Carnforth Hall.

Just then Doug's head slumped onto Christy's shoulder, immediately waking him. "Oh, I'm sorry. I must have fallen asleep."

"That's okay," Christy said. "Why don't you get some more sleep? You can use my shoulder if you need a pillow."

Doug's little-boy grin spread across his groggy face. "How come you're still awake? Those two look like they fell asleep as fast as I did."

"There's too much to see," Christy said, smiling back at Doug. "This is all so amazing to me. I don't want to miss anything."

Without drawing attention to her actions, Christy closed her diary and slid it back into her shoulder bag. It wasn't that she had anything to hide from Doug. She just didn't have anything she wanted to share. Her diary was her collection of private thoughts, and as much as she liked Doug, she didn't want to let him into those thoughts.

"You hungry?" Doug asked.

Christy let out a gentle laugh. She knew Doug was hungry. He was always hungry. "I could go for a cup of tea."

"You're becoming quite the little tea drinker, aren't you?" Doug yawned and stretched both his long legs into the aisle. "I think I'll go find that snack bar or whatever they call it and see if they have any sandwiches. You want a candy bar or something to go with your tea?"

Christy shrugged. "Doesn't matter." Then with a friendly tease in her voice she said, "I'm sure you'll eat whatever I can't finish."

"I'll get two candy bars then. Maybe three," Doug said, standing in the aisle and reaching for his backpack under the seat.

"Do you need some money?" Christy asked. "Mine is right here."

"No, I've got it." He balanced his way down the narrow aisle and through the doors into the next car on the train.

What a sweetheart. He really is an incredible guy. Christy sighed and looked out the window.

The train was slowing to a stop at a small-town train station. On the wooden landing stood a lad wearing a black cap, knee socks, shorts, and a dark blazer. He held a closed umbrella in one hand and a briefcase-looking book satchel in the other. He stood completely still as the train chugged out of the station. Christy watched him through her wide window with a smile. In her imagination, he was Peter, brother of Susan, Edmund, and Lucy in C. S. Lewis' British fantasy series *The Chronicles of Narnia.* Christy was sure "Peter" was about to enter an invisible door into Narnia.

"Your tea, miss," Doug said, startling her back to the real world.

He placed a large paper cup covered with a plastic lid on the table before her and handed her several tiny plastic cream containers and packets of sugar. In his hand was a medium-sized paper bag with a handle.

Doug looked cute. He had swaggered away as a long-legged man and trotted back as a shy boy with a picnic basket in his hand. He sat next to Christy and reached into the lunch bag.

"Ham and cheese," he said, producing two wrapped sandwiches. "And Toblerone." Christy recognized the long, triangular-shaped box that held a candy bar. She had seen some on sale at a newsstand in London.

"They call candy bars 'sweeties' here," Doug informed her. "At least that's what the guy at the lunch window said. It's kind of hard not to crack up when a grown man looks you in the eye and says, 'Would you like a sweetie?' "

Christy giggled and poured her cream and sugar into her hot cup of tea.

"I should have told the guy I already had a sweetie," Doug said.

Their eyes met. Christy smiled her thanks and then looked away.

Why do I feel embarrassed? This is Doug. My boyfriend. Why does it still feel awkward when he says nice things to me?

Christy didn't have time to come to a conclusion because just then Tracy woke up and said, "Are we almost to Manchester?" It was as if she had invaded their private moment, and yet somehow Christy felt relieved.

"No. About another hour, I'd guess," Doug said, chomping into his sandwich. "You want a bite, Trace?"

With a yawn she answered, "No, thanks. I could use a bathroom, though. Do you know which way it is?"

"That way," Doug said, pointing in the direction from which he had just come. "Only they call it a 'W.C.' Stands for 'Water Closet,' I think."

"Katie," Tracy said, gently nudging the sleeping redhead. "Sorry, Katie, but I need to get out."

Katie groaned and reluctantly lifted her head. With an annoyed look, she moved to the aisle so Tracy could slide by.

"Thanks," Tracy said before hurrying down the aisle.

"Why don't you slide over by the window so you won't have to move again when she comes back?" Christy suggested.

"All her junk is there," Katie said.

"So? Move it. She won't mind."

With exaggerated movements, Katie plopped Tracy's things onto the top of the table, jiggling Christy's cup of tea and nearly causing it to spill. Then Katie scooted over and curled up with her head against the window, closing her eyes and tuning them out.

Doug and Christy exchanged glances, but neither of them made a comment. Christy hated this feeling. She wished that everyone could just get along and not become upset with each other. But life didn't tend to be like that.

And she wasn't so innocent herself. She had had her share of conflicts with friends and grumpy comments that she had later regretted. Christy decided it would be best to leave Katie alone and pray for grace and peace and concord for the remainder of the trip. It would be great if Katie and Tracy could recognize their similarities and work at using them together, as a team, instead of turning against each other.

"How's the tea?" Doug asked, obviously trying to redirect the focus.

"Good. Really good. Thanks."

Doug looked at his watch. "We should be right on schedule, which means we'll have about an hour to settle into our rooms at the castle before the evening meal."

"Is it a real castle?" Christy asked. "I thought that's just what they called it, but then Tracy said some guy bought it after World War II and turned it into a Christian retreat center for teens."

"That's right. The guy bought this old castle and something like five hundred acres. He wanted the youth of Europe to unite after the war and thought the best way to do that would be to bring them together for summer Bible camps. They would get saved and go back to their countries equipped to share the Gospel."

"That's pretty amazing," Christy said. "This whole outreach program to different parts of Europe amazes me too."

"I'm looking forward to meeting the rest of the group to-night," Doug said in between bites of his second sandwich. "The last I heard, there are going to be about forty students from all over the world. They'll divide us up into groups of eight on a team."

"Do you think the four of us will be together?" Christy asked.

"That's what I requested. I think they'll probably keep us together."

Christy was thinking it might be better if Tracy and Katie were split up. She didn't let her thoughts out in the open, though somehow, by the look on Doug's face, she had a feeling he was thinking the same thing.

Later that evening, at their opening meeting in Carnforth Hall, Doug's prediction was confirmed. When the director read the team lists aloud, Doug, Tracy, Christy, and Katie were all together with three other guys and one more girl. Their team assignment was Belfast, Northern Ireland.

"I don't believe it," Katie said under her breath to Christy. "That's exactly where I wanted to go. This is perfect! I feel as if I already know about Belfast from everything Michael told me last year."

Christy remained silent as the rest of the assignments were announced. It was fine for Katie to feel good about the assignment because she had dated a guy from Belfast, but Christy felt disappointed. Or was she a little frightened? Belfast wasn't where she expected to go. She didn't know where she expected to go. Sweden, maybe? Or Spain? Ireland didn't feel right.

"Find the rest of your team members," the director, Charles Benson, said. "We'll gather back in this room in one hour."

Doug's name had been listed as the team captain, and he immediately began his role as organizer by calling out, "Belfast! Who's on the Belfast team?"

Other team leaders began to do the same, calling out their cities. "Barcelona, over here." "Oslo." "Amsterdam." "Edinburgh!" It sounded like an international train station, as chairs were shuffled and everyone began to mingle.

Christy felt overwhelmed for the first time on the trip. Perhaps jet lag was finally catching up with her, or maybe it was reality catching up. She was standing in an ornately decorated drawing room in an old English castle. After a week's training, she would be on her way to Belfast. It hit her like a gust of wind, nearly knocking the breath out of her.

"Okay, great! Belfast is all together. Let's grab those chairs over there by the windows," Doug said.

They weren't just windows. They were castle windows, six

long columns reaching to the high ceiling with ornate woodwork laced along the top. The thick, floral drapes hung to the floor. The blue couch and chairs in front of the window were ordinary enough, which was a good thing. Christy was beginning to feel the way Katie had in Charles Dickens' home: new-experience sensory overload.

"I'm Doug, and this is Christy, Katie, and Tracy. We're all from southern California," Doug said once the eight of them were seated. "Why don't you guys introduce yourselves?"

"I'm Sierra," the girl next to Tracy said. "I'm also from California, but I'm from northern California. Pineville. I know you've never heard of it. No one has. It's a very small mountain community near Lake Tahoe. I grew up there, but while I'm on this trip my family is moving to Portland, Oregon. So I'm sort of from California still."

Christy immediately liked her. She had wild, wavy, caramel-colored hair, a freckled nose, and a natural, approachable demeanor. There was an earthy, honest quality about her that was reflected in her jeans, cowboy boots, and brown leather jacket. Somehow, on her, the outfit worked. Even her unusual name seemed like a perfect fit.

"I'm Gernot," said a tall, thin guy with a definite accent. "I'm from Austria. My home is not far from Salzburg."

"My name is Ian, and I'm from England, but I'm living now in Germany." Ian reminded Christy of a professor, with his thin nose, wire-rimmed glasses, and thick gray wool sweater.

"And I'm Stephen. I also live in Germany, where I am going to school with Ian. And I'd like to say we must have the best team here since all of our girls are from America." He smiled, and his previously somber face turned into a splash of sunshine. His dark hair was combed straight back, and he had a goatee, which made

Stephen seem older than the rest of their group.

For the get-acquainted hour, each of them told why he or she had come on the trip. Katie seemed to come alive, with her animated description of her motivations for coming and why Belfast was the perfect place for their outreach. The two German guys seemed thoroughly entertained.

Christy stammered a bit when it was her turn to share. She said she wanted to find out what God had for her life and if maybe missions should be a part of it. Aside from that, she couldn't give much more of an explanation. The trip seemed like a great idea when Doug suggested it, and the money had come in on time, so she thought she should go.

"My reason is kind of the same," Sierra said. "It all worked out. I guess I needed to get a dose of the big world out there that I've never seen. I don't know what I want to be when I grow up, and I'm hoping this trip will help give me some direction."

Now Christy knew she really liked Sierra. She felt as if she'd just discovered a kindred spirit. Christy smiled at her. Sierra smiled back. Their friendship was sealed.

CHAPTER FIVE

Knights on White Steeds

It didn't really hit Christy where she was until the next morning. She woke up before the alarm sounded and, through bleary eyes, gazed around the second-floor dorm room. The seven other girls who shared her room were all still asleep.

I'm in England. I'm in a castle. I'm not dreaming.

She remembered a wish she had made at summer camp two years ago while in a canoe in the middle of a lake. She had said she wished she could go to England someday and visit a castle. And now, poof! Here she was in England, and for the next week, this castle was her home.

Christy stuck her legs out of bed and padded to the window on stockinged feet. It had been cold last night. Despite her warm sweats and thick socks, she had felt a damp chill while trying to fall asleep. Now, tiptoeing to the frosted windowpane, she caught her first daytime view of the grounds surrounding Carnforth Hall. Even through the frost, the world beyond her window was beautiful. Storybook-like.

She gazed at the acres of icy green meadows stretching out below her. Gnarled trees lifted their leafless branches toward the gray sky, and thick moss clung to the tree trunks and fence posts.

A fine mist enveloped the entire scene, making it look like an impressionist painter's work. It was all so different from the warm beach climate at home. She loved it.

"Beautiful, isn't it?" Sierra whispered over Christy's shoulder. Christy jumped. She hadn't heard Sierra approach. Christy nodded and smiled.

Sierra stood a few inches away. She wore her blanket wrapped around her shoulders like an Indian maiden and stared out the window with a contented look on her face. "I'm so glad I'm here."

"Me too," Christy whispered back. "I'm glad you're here too."

"This is going to be quite an experience, isn't it?"

Just then someone's alarm went off, and a groping arm shot out from under a blanket and slapped at the bedside table several times before hitting its mark.

"What time is it?" Tracy called from her burrow beneath the warm blankets.

"Six-thirty," came the muffled response from the alarm slammer. "Breakfast is in an hour."

"Don't you wish they would serve us hot tea in our rooms?" Sierra asked with a giggle.

"I know," Christy agreed. "That would sure take the edge off this morning chill. I can't bear the thought of having to take off these sweats to get dressed! I just want to add more layers and put on my boots."

"Why not?" Sierra said, her freckled nose scrunching up. "You could start a fashion trend. It sounds pretty practical. It might catch on."

Christy decided against starting a new trend and managed to quickly change into her leggings, her warmest black pants, several layers on the top, and two pairs of wool socks. Castles may look enchanting, but Christy decided they can be freezing!

The group assembled for breakfast, all forty of them, in a small dining room. A large chandelier and three up-to-the-ceiling windows brightened their morning meal. Christy was happy to see a pot of hot tea already placed at the center of each table with a small jug of milk and a bowl of sugar.

Doug sat next to her, wearing his favorite green and blue rugby shirt with a white turtleneck underneath. Tracy joined them, her short hair perfectly holding its shape and her cheeks looking especially pink. She sat across the table from them, and after the prayer and a song, Doug asked Tracy her opinion on how to organize the team, which she gladly gave in her sweet, well-thought-out manner.

It bugged Christy that Doug hadn't asked her opinion. However, if he had, she wouldn't have known what to say. She hadn't thought about it at all. Obviously Tracy had.

Doug used Tracy's ideas when their team met after breakfast. "Before we get going, I wonder if each of you would feel comfortable giving your testimony. You know, say a little bit about how you became a Christian, what God has been doing in your life since then, and what your spiritual gifts are, if you know. Who would like to start?"

Each member of the group told his or her story. All were different and interesting. Christy was the last to share.

"My family always went to church, and my parents are Christians. I guess I knew all about God, only it was as if He were all around me, but not inside me, if you know what I mean."

Christy told about meeting Todd, Doug, and Tracy on the beach the summer she turned fifteen. She explained how Tracy and Todd gave her a Bible for her birthday. It was nice having Tracy right there as sort of a visual aid for her testimony.

"Then the day after my birthday . . . well, some stuff had happened that made me realize I needed God to be more than just someone who was watching me from a distance. So I surrendered my life to Him. I guess that's the best way of saying it. I just gave everything to God and asked for His forgiveness for my sins. I promised Him my heart. My whole heart. Forever."

Christy didn't expect the tears, but suddenly they were there, filling her eyes. Doug reached over and gave her a comforting hug. Her mind flashed back to the night after she had given her life to the Lord. Doug was sitting beside her by the campfire on the beach that night too. He was the first one of their crowd to congratulate her on becoming a Christian, and his hug that night had felt just as warm and reassuring as his hug did this morning.

Something bothered Christy, though. Something deep inside. She knew her tears came from something other than joy. They had been swallowed long ago, maybe not all at once, but slowly. Deliberately. Stuffed deep inside her heart.

She wanted to leave the room, run outside, go for a long walk, and dig to the bottom of her emotional treasure chest until she found where those tears came from.

The rest of the group apparently thought she was moved by the miracle of her salvation, because all of them began to give words of comfort and reassurance. Everyone but Sierra.

Sierra's testimony had been straightforward enough. She grew up in a Christian home, asked Jesus into her heart when she was five one night in her bedroom with her mom, and had been a good girl ever since. Could it be there was something in Sierra's heart that connected with Christy's?

Christy stayed in her seat and participated with the rest of the group in planning out the first stage of their training. Her soul-searching would have to wait. Their preliminary assignment was

a week away, next Saturday. They were to plan a day-long outreach in a small town nearby. In conjunction with the church that
was hosting their team, they were to present a drama, some
music, a program for the children, and an evening message. This
was a miniature version of the kind of ministry they would be
doing in Belfast with a local church.

Katie immediately volunteered to head up the drama, and
Sierra and Stephen jumped in, saying drama was their area of interest as well. Since Doug was the only one who could play a guitar, he accepted responsibility for the music. Tracy offered to help
him. Ian, who looked the part of a professor, wanted to try his
hand at the evening message. Gernot suggested that he head up
a game of soccer with the boys of the town to draw them in for
the evening meeting. All that was left for Christy was the children's program. That was fine. She had worked many hours in the
toddler Sunday school at her church, and she liked little kids.

"That was easy," Doug said, checking his watch. "Well, we
have morning chapel in about fifteen minutes. I'll try to hunt up
an extra guitar around here. Our team has lunch duty, so go to
the kitchen right after chapel."

Christy was glad the chapel was in a different building. It
meant bundling up and taking an umbrella, but the walk helped
clear her head a bit.

Even in the frost, the garden seemed beautiful to her. Neat
rows of trimmed rose bushes lined the walkway. She was sure that
in the spring and summer this would be her favorite place. She
passed under an arched trellis with some kind of barren vine
woven through the latticework. She thought of the fragrant jasmine that climbed up the posts by her front porch at home, and
for the first time, she missed her mom, dad, and little brother. She

had sent them a postcard from London. Today would be a good day to write a real letter.

The chapel was situated at the end of the garden walkway. The fine, old stone building had once served as a church for the castle's household.

Entering the chapel through the thick wooden doors, Christy felt the same reverent awe she had experienced at Westminster Abbey. For hundreds of years this spot had been a place of prayer and worship, and now she was one of the many who had entered in and sought the Lord.

Christy sat alone on a solid wooden pew about halfway toward the front. Instead of an altar at the front, there was a stage with microphones and a keyboard. At first glance it seemed out of place. But within a few minutes the chapel began to fill with other students, and several musicians stepped up on the stage to begin to tune their instruments.

"Are you saving this seat for anyone?" a girl with a big smile and very short, blond hair asked. She wore a sweatshirt that said, *"Aika on kala."* Christy couldn't begin to guess what language that was.

"No," Christy automatically said, not even thinking that Doug might have expected her to save him a seat. "My name's Christy."

"I'm Merja. I'm from Finland. Where are you from?"

"The United States. California."

"Really? Do you surf and drive a convertible?" Merja asked with a teasing smile.

"You've been watching too much TV," Christy said.

"You live in Beverly Hills, don't you?" Merja asked, still teasing.

"Not exactly," Christy said. "However, I do know several guys who surf, and my aunt and uncle used to own a convertible. Does that count?"

"Close enough," Merja said. "We can be friends now. I'm on the team going to Barcelona. Where are you going?"

For the next few minutes, the two new friends enjoyed a lively conversation. Christy was enjoying this opportunity to make friends with people from all over the world.

When she glanced up on the stage, she noticed Doug standing there, guitar in hand, tuning up with the rest of the band.

"Let's start off with some praise choruses," the group leader said. "This first one is from Psalm 5."

The singing sounded majestic in the small chapel. It was the first time Christy had felt like everyone was part of one group as they sang these familiar choruses, all in English but with a variety of accents.

Doug kept up with the rest of the band. Apparently he knew all the chords to all the songs they played. At one point he looked up and cast his little-boy grin into the crowd. She thought he was smiling at her, but the look seemed to go over her head. Christy slowly looked over her shoulder between songs and noticed Tracy sitting two rows behind her.

Oh, it's Tracy.

Now she wondered where Katie was, and if everything was cleared up between the two of them. She guessed it would become evident as the week went on.

She didn't have to wait long to see. After chapel their team assembled in the kitchen. Within two minutes, Katie and Tracy were disagreeing over how the tables should be set.

Mrs. Bates, the white-aproned cook, stepped in and made it clear. "Knife only on the right side. Fork only on the left side. The spoon goes above the plate, like this."

"But that's not how we do it at home," Katie protested.

"You are *not* at home," Mrs. Bates said firmly. With a twinkle of good humor in her voice, she added, "This is how we do it here. And for this week, this is your home, and I am your mother, so mind your mother!"

Tracy had every right to say "I told you so" to Katie. But she said nothing and calmly went about setting her tables while Katie walked around her table, resetting each place with the spoon above the plate.

Suddenly Katie blurted out, "You guys, I'm sorry. I don't know why I'm being like this. I keep trying to make everything familiar, and it's not. It all seems so weird to me."

Oh no, there she goes with the weird thing again!

Christy thought Tracy would arch her back like a cat. She didn't. Instead she quietly stepped over to Katie and said, "I know. It's not easy fitting into another culture, is it?"

"I don't see you having such a problem with it. I don't see anyone else having a hard time." Katie waved her handful of knives around the room. "It's just me. I don't fit in here."

Doug had proven to be a wonderful counselor more than once to Katie. He stepped in and, putting his arm around her, said, "Can we talk in the other room, Katie? I think these guys can set the table without you."

Katie let her knives drop loudly onto the table. "Yeah, they'll do a better job without me." She walked out of the dining room with Doug's arm still around her.

The rest of the team went about their lunch duties without saying much.

Tracy came up to Christy and said, "Could I talk to you sometime?"

"Sure," Christy answered. "Right after lunch."

Lunch was the main meal every day, and today it was sau
sages, scalloped potatoes, and once again, mushy peas. Doug and
Katie had returned to the dining room in time to eat, and even
though they sat across the room, Christy could tell Katie had
been crying.

As soon as the team had finished their cleanup duties, Tracy
and Christy headed for a sequestered nook with a padded bench
seat. A tall, arched window beside them opened up a view of the
lawn that stretched all the way down to the brook. Beyond that
was the forest.

"I wanted to ask you something," Tracy said.

Christy liked Tracy, with her gentle yet direct manner. The
two had shared many meaningful conversations over the years,
and this felt as if it were going to be one of those heart-to-heart
talks.

"What can I do to change things with Katie? I feel awful. I
thought London would be so fun with you guys. And it was, in a
way. But the whole time I felt as if Katie were mad at me. I don't
know what to do."

Christy tried to accurately represent one friend to another.
She found it wasn't easy. "I know Katie doesn't want to be acting,
well . . . for lack of a better word, 'weird.' I guess this trip is harder
for her than she thought it would be. I don't think it's you, Tracy.
I think it's everything being so different. This doesn't seem to be
Katie's cup of tea, so to speak. I know she's trying, though. I don't
think you could do anything differently than you've been doing
it."

"Every time I open my mouth, I seem to offend her," Tracy
said. "I don't know what the problem is. What do you think I
should do?"

"I think you two should talk. You're both special friends to me, and I'll be honest, it has bothered me that things have been tense. I think the two of you should sit down and talk."

"Do you want to be there?"

"I don't think that would help. It would be better if it were just the two of you."

Tracy let out a sigh. "I guess you're right. I'll try to talk to her this afternoon. Pray for us, okay?"

"I will." Christy squeezed Tracy's hand, and the two friends sat silently for a few minutes on the tapestry-covered seat, gazing out the window.

"Can't you just picture some princess sitting at this very seat hundreds of years ago, waiting for her prince to ride up on his white horse and whisk her away to the ends of the earth?" Christy said, swooping her hand through the air in a dramatic gesture.

"You don't have to wait for your prince," Tracy said with temperate, steady words.

"What do you mean?" Christy asked.

Tracy looked at her with disbelief. "You know, Doug? That prince-type of a guy? Your knight on a white steed has already arrived."

"Oh, yeah," Christy said. She felt embarrassed and surprised that she hadn't even been thinking about Doug. "I meant, you know, some princess long ago. I wasn't thinking about you and me and our princes."

The minute the words were out, Christy wished she could reel them back in. There was no prince in Tracy's life. There hadn't been for a long time.

Christy decided to probe a little. "How are things in the prince department for you, anyhow? Did anything ever work out with that guy from college you mentioned at Christmas?"

"No, that fizzled."

"So there's nobody you're interested in?" Christy asked.

Tracy paused. By the expression on her heart-shaped face, Christy could tell she was carefully pondering her answer. Tracy couldn't lie. She always told the truth, which made it difficult for her when she was cornered with a question.

"I didn't say there's nobody I'm interested in. However, I've learned over my vast years of experience that it simply works better when he's interested in me as well."

"Wait a minute," Christy said. "I distinctly remember having this same sort of conversation with you once before. Don't you remember? We were making cookies at my aunt and uncle's house. You liked somebody then, but you wouldn't tell me who it was."

If Tracy did remember the conversation, she didn't appear to be willing to comment on it or on her current interest.

Christy prodded her along. "Don't you remember that afternoon at my aunt and uncle's? You didn't tell me then, but I figured out later that you liked Doug."

Tracy nodded.

"Can you believe you guys used to go out?" Christy asked. "Doesn't that seem like a lifetime ago?"

Tracy's expression changed a little. "I guess it does. That was more than three years ago, and we only dated for a few months."

"Why did you guys break up?"

Now Tracy paused longer. "What has Doug told you?"

"Nothing. We've never talked about it," Christy said.

"Maybe it's best we leave it that way," Tracy said.

"You know," Christy said after a pause, "this thing Doug has about how he's never kissed a girl and how his first kiss will be at the altar on his wedding day? Well, it's made our relationship different because I don't wonder about his past girlfriends or what went on with them. It's really freeing. He's never kissed me, and that takes all the pressure off. I don't wonder if he's going to or not. Do you know what I mean? Of course you know what I mean."

Tracy looked out the window, seemingly lost in thought. "Um-hmm," she agreed.

"It's just different," Christy said. "It makes it easy for us to all be friends."

"Um-hmm," Tracy agreed again.

The two friends sat together silently, each lost in her own world of thoughts and dreams.

CHAPTER SIX

Communion and Concord

Sunday morning church service was in the chapel. The mission director, Charles Benson, introduced the group doing the music. "And now, Undivided will lead in morning worship."

The name struck Christy as ironic. Tracy and Katie had not yet talked, and in their room this morning it was obvious the tension was growing. Now at the morning service, Christy sat next to Tracy while Katie was on the other side of the chapel with two of the guys from their team. Sierra sat on the other side of Christy, and Doug was on the end of the aisle, next to Tracy. Their team was quickly becoming anything *but* undivided.

The tension made it hard for Christy to concentrate as they sang and even harder to take the message for herself. Everything seemed to apply to Katie, not her.

Dr. Benson spoke on John 17. "Did you know that Christ actually prayed for us? Look at verse 21. Here Christ prayed that we might be one, just as He and the Father are one. This is usually the biggest challenge for ministry teams. Each of you is coming from a different background, with different opinions and points of view. It's not easy to be 'one.' One heart. One mind. One undivided team."

Christy thought Dr. Benson must know what was going on with their team, even though he seemed to speak to the whole group. He then talked about forgiveness and starting over. He urged the teams to learn how to exercise grace and peace.

It made Christy think of the inscription she'd written in her diary on the train. Grace and peace and what was that word for harmony? Concord. That's what they needed. Grace, peace, and concord. At this moment it seemed impossible.

"I'm going to ask you to do something you may never have done before," Dr. Benson said. "We're going to take communion this morning, and we need to come before God with clean hearts. Some of you need to be reconciled with your brothers and sisters in this room. Before we serve communion, we will have ten minutes in which, if you need to ask someone for forgiveness, you should do so. It would be utterly false to take part in communion and then be commissioned for your outreach trips if any of you is harboring unforgiveness in your heart."

Christy closed her eyes and searched her heart. She wanted to make sure she was right with God in every way. Plenty of small things needed to be confessed, things between her and God. But she didn't think she needed to go to anyone and ask forgiveness.

As Christy silently prayed, she heard Katie's voice behind her saying, "Tracy, could I talk to you for a minute?"

Tracy slipped past Doug, and Christy peeked to see the two of them walk to the back of the chapel and speak quietly with each other. She wanted to listen in. She felt thrilled the two of them were patching things up.

Just then Doug slid over on the pew next to Christy and, leaning over to whisper in her ear, he said, "Christy, will you please forgive me?"

She was caught off guard. "For what?" she whispered back.

Doug hesitated and seemed to have a hard time finding the words. "I haven't been, well, I guess I haven't been honoring you the way I should."

Christy wasn't sure what he meant. She looked up at his face for a clue. He looked distraught about something. "Of course I forgive you. Have I done anything that's bothered you?"

"No, no. Of course not." Doug looked relieved. He smiled at her and said, "Life can get complicated sometimes, can't it?"

Christy nodded and returned the smile he was giving her, even though she still wasn't sure what he was talking about. Perhaps he meant complicated with Tracy and Katie, and he felt he should have been more understanding of Christy since she was caught in the middle. Whatever the situation was, it didn't matter.

Tracy and Katie were returning to the pew now, both teary-eyed and with humble expressions. Doug scooted over closer to Christy to make room for the two of them on the end of the bench. Christy let out a tiny sigh of relief and bowed her head, waiting for the communion to be served.

It was the most meaningful communion she had ever participated in. After that, they all stood, and the mission director and several staff members prayed for the forty and commissioned them to go forth on their outreaches next Saturday. When the service was over, Doug asked that their team stick around for a few minutes. Once they were all together, he asked if anyone had anything he or she wanted to say. It seemed as if they were all trying not to look at Katie, or at least to wait until she said something before they looked at her.

"I need to apologize to all of you guys," Katie said.

All eyes quickly focused on her. "I've learned a lot these past few days, and God has been teaching me some stuff I didn't want to learn. I've been trying to hold on to a lot of things. It's like I had this fistful of stuff I didn't want to give to God, and He's been patiently trying to pry back each of my fingers to get the garbage out of there." Katie held out her hand and demonstrated God's imaginary hand pulling at her clenched fingers.

"All I can say is that I'd like to start over, with a new attitude of being open to God and open to you guys. Tracy has forgiven me, and now I want to say to the rest of you, I'm sorry I've been such a jerk. I hope you guys can all forgive me too."

A chorus of yeses responded to Katie.

"You're among friends, Katie," Sierra said. "It's never too late to start over." She gave Katie a hug, and the rest of the group followed.

"I think we should pray," Doug said. "Let's pray right now that our team will be knit together in love, like Dr. Benson was saying. We need to be of one mind and heart."

They all prayed. It was as if a huge breath of fresh air blew over them. They left the chapel with arms around each other, laughing and high stepping their way to the dining room. Christy tried not to think about Doug's comment. It was past. Over. She had forgiven him—for whatever it was.

That afternoon they had four hours of free time, and Christy thought it would be fun to go for a long walk with Doug. She sidled up to him after their meal time. He was talking with Tracy, and Christy asked if either or both of them wanted to go for a walk with her.

"Maybe a little bit later," Doug said. "Tracy and I need to work on our music for the outreach."

"You guys could go now if you want to, Doug," Tracy said quickly. "We can practice another time."

It was silent for an awkward minute before Christy said, "No, that's fine. You guys don't have much time to practice. We can go for a walk later. It doesn't matter, really."

"Are you sure?" Doug asked, turning to face Christy and look-ing into her eyes.

"Of course, I'm sure. You guys need time to practice. Have fun, okay?" Christy said sincerely. Then she willingly received Doug's hug.

"I'll come looking for you later," he said.

"Okay." Now Christy wasn't sure what to do. She wanted to go for a walk by herself, yet she thought a nap sounded good. What she didn't want to do was feel sorry for herself. Not after that communion service and the way the team had started to come together.

She decided to go to her room and headed down the hallway. The sound of laughter drew her into the great drawing room. Some of the Barcelona team was gathered around the huge marble fireplace, where a great orange fire crackled and warmed the whole room.

Merja spotted Christy and called her over to their group. "We need one more player. Will you be on our team?"

Spread before them on the low coffee table was some sort of word game Christy had seen before but had never played. Joining a group of laughing friends seemed much more appealing than the quiet, close quarters of the chilly dorm room.

"Sure, but I've never played this before." Christy wedged in on the rug next to Merja and tucked her long legs underneath her. Merja made quick introductions of the other players. Christy was teamed up with Merja and another girl from Finland named Satu. She said her name in English meant "fairy tale," and then she burst out laughing.

"It really does," Satu said. "No one here believes me."

"I believe you," Christy said.

"And what does your name mean?" Satu asked Christy.

"It means 'follower of Christ.' "

"How perfect!" Satu flipped her long blond hair behind her right ear and said, "I'm glad to have an American to play this English game with. English is really my fourth language, and it is not my best."

"What other languages do you speak?" Christy asked.

"Finnish, Spanish, Italian, and then English. I know some Russian and some German, but not much." Satu didn't throw her list out in a bragging way. She almost seemed to apologize that her English wasn't better. To Christy's ear it sounded perfect.

The game began, and within five minutes, Christy was laughing so hard the tears were skipping down her cheeks. It was the first time she had laughed that hard since she left home. There had been some funny moments in London, but the tension and exhaustion had made the first four or five days of this trip strained. For the next few hours, she, Merja, Satu, and the others laughed. It was like medicine.

She didn't see Doug again until the evening meal. Christy was sitting next to Satu when Doug and Tracy walked in. She waved at them, but they didn't seem to notice her and slipped into two open seats at a table by the door. After dinner a prayer and praise meeting was held in the chapel. It lasted for nearly two hours, with singing and praying. Christy loved it, but now this growing mysterious feeling about Doug was really bothering her.

After the evening worship, their team went as a group to the dining room for cake and hot chocolate. Doug was standing next to Sierra with a cup of cocoa in his hand when Christy decided it was time to get his attention.

"Could I talk to you a minute, Doug?" she asked, surprised that her voice came out shaky.

"Sure." He turned his full attention to her, looking surprised at her expression. "Is something wrong?"

"May I have your attention, please?" Dr. Benson stood in the doorway. "The hour draws to a close, and you need to be in your rooms in ten minutes."

A group groan leaked out across the room.

"I know, I know," the good-natured Dr. Benson said. "But good soldiers are disciplined, and this is your opportunity to exercise that discipline. Tomorrow is a full day, starting with breakfast at 7:30. I need to see all the team leaders for a moment in the hallway. May you all experience the truth of Proverbs 3:24, 'When you lie down, your sleep will be sweet.' Good night. See you all in the morning."

"We'll talk tomorrow, okay?" Doug said, placing his cup down on the table and making his way to the hallway to meet with the other team leaders.

Christy swallowed her disappointment and walked up the stairs to their room with Sierra by her side. She hated it when these clouds of moodiness hovered over her like the morning mist on the fields outside her castle window. She tried to shake off her thoughts and pay attention to what Sierra was saying.

"Doesn't it seem as if we've been here months and months instead of only a few days?"

"Sort of," Christy answered.

Sierra kept up the friendly chatter even after they were ready for bed. She wrapped herself up in her blanket and curled up at the foot of Christy's bed while the other girls finished their bedtime preparations. It was fun getting to know Sierra. Christy liked her more each day and was glad they were on the same team.

Katie wrapped herself in a blanket and joined them, laughing as she tried to repeat a joke one of the guys from Sweden had told her at dinner. Tracy crawled into her bed, which was directly across from Christy's, and listened in on the conversation.

"I don't get it," Tracy said when Katie finished the joke and laughed joyfully.

Katie repeated the punch line. "She come on a Honda."

Still none of them laughed.

"I guess it was one of those you-had-to-be-there kind of jokes. Leo is really hilarious. I wish he were on our team."

"I think our team is perfect," Sierra said. "Or were you hoping for guys who were a bit more promising as future spouse material?"

Christy liked being all curled up with her friends and having a "boy talk." It felt like a slumber party from her high school days. It was especially good to see Katie back to her old self, relaxed and getting along with everyone.

"Our guys are pretty cool," Katie said. "They're kind of quiet, though. I like guys who are a bit more on the rowdy side."

"Not me," Tracy said. "I prefer the strong, leader type. You know, the kind of guy who tries to make everyone feel welcome and who doesn't draw a lot of attention to himself."

"That sounds like Doug," Sierra said, brushing back a wild curl of hair that had fallen onto her forehead. "Come to think of it, you and Doug would make a perfect couple. Why aren't you going after Doug?"

Katie, Tracy, and Christy greeted the question with silence. "What? What did I say? Is there something wrong with Doug? I think he's a great guy. You two would be good together with your personalities, your gifts, your interests. You would make a cute couple. What's wrong with that?"

"There's only one slight problem," Katie volunteered. "Doug happens to be Christy's boyfriend."

"You're kidding," Sierra said, scanning Christy's face for verification.

Christy didn't say anything. She bit her lower lip. How should she respond?

"I'm sorry," Sierra said quickly. "I just never would have guessed. And maybe that's a good thing. You guys don't exclude anyone else. You act like friends, and he seems to treat you the same way he does the other girls, and well . . . I just didn't know."

"The three of us *are* all good friends," Katie explained. "We've known each other a long time, and Doug did go out with Tracy for a while, but that was a long time ago, right, Tracy?"

Tracy nodded.

"See, Christy used to go out with this surfer named Todd. You know the type, tall, blond, blue-eyed, incredibly strong Christian," Katie said.

"Sounds too good to be true," Sierra said.

"Exactly," Katie agreed. "And Todd just so happened to be best friends with Doug." She adjusted her cross-legged position and proceeded to fill Sierra in on Christy's dating history as if Christy weren't there. It would have bothered Christy, except everything Katie said was true, and somehow it was less agonizing to hear it all from Katie than to try and explain it herself.

Right at the part in the saga in which Todd received a letter from a mission organization last spring asking him to join their staff full-time, a knock at the door reminded the girls it was time for lights out. They switched off the lights. Tracy pulled her bed over next to Christy's, and Katie continued her story, whispering in the dark.

When she finished, Sierra asked, "So Tracy, why did you and Doug break up?"

Tracy didn't answer for a long time. "I don't think it really matters. Like Katie said, that was a long time ago, and Christy and Doug are together now. I know Doug has wanted to go out with Christy for years. That may have had something to do with how he felt about me even while we were dating."

"This is a soap opera, you guys," Sierra said. "I never would have guessed any of this. Where is this Todd guy now?"

"Who knows?" Christy said.

"You really don't know? He never wrote any of you?"

"Doug heard from him once or twice," Tracy said. "But Todd is rather independent. He's doing what he always wanted to do, probably on some South Seas island somewhere. It's not much of a surprise to any of us."

"My next question," Sierra said. "Tracy? Katie? Are either of you interested in any of the guys here?"

"I'll tell you about my interest in guys," Katie said. "I've come to a conclusion after spending so many years of my life trying not to be jealous of Christy because she's always had some guy interested in her. I don't even try anymore. We didn't even tell you about Rick. Now *that* was a bizarre guy. I tried to get Rick interested in me for a while. Boy, was that a mistake. Rick turned out to be such a loser. I heard he moved in with some girl, and he totally fell away from whatever kind of relationship he had with the Lord."

"I still feel bad about that," Christy said.

"It certainly wasn't your fault," Katie said.

"I know, but I still wish he hadn't walked away from the Lord."

"It's hard," Sierra agreed.

"Then there was Michael," Katie continued. "That was another whole era in my life. Michael was from Belfast, so that's one good thing that came from our relationship. I'm probably more interested in Belfast than anyone else on the team. Anyway, my new motto is 'Seek pals only.' I am so far from being ready for a romance, it isn't even funny."

"I feel the same way," Sierra said.

"In a way," Katie said, "I'm trying to go back and make up for all those dumb years I spent in high school trying so hard to get a boyfriend and missing out on some great friendships. I learned a lot about non-romantic friendships with this guy, Fred, that I went to my senior prom with. Of course, Fred was also crazy about Christy for a long time, and he only took me to the prom because she turned him down. Still, Fred is my pal. I'm only interested in finding more pals here and trying to grow up a little bit emotionally before I consider anything more in a relationship with a guy."

"That is exactly how I feel," Sierra agreed. "I couldn't have said it better myself. Isn't it funny how backwards we are? This is what we should have been doing back in middle school, and here we are, half grown up and just now trying to figure out how to be friends with guys. All I can say is I'm sure glad God didn't answer all my prayers regarding some of the guys I've been interested in over the past few years."

"Amen!" Katie said. "If you ask me, Tracy, you're ahead of all of us in the being-friends-with-guys department. You're also older than the three of us."

"I'm also probably more desirous of a romance at this point in my life, and that's not an easy thing to live with." Tracy's whispered confession carried a hint of sadness. "I'd love to get married as soon as I finish college, settle down, and have a couple of kids while I'm still young. And in a way, I feel ready for that phase of my life. However, there does seem to be one thing missing."

"Mr. Right," Sierra answered for her.

"You guessed it," Tracy said.

Sierra leaned forward and said, "Who knows, Tracy. Mr. Right might be here this week, and you had to come all the way to England to meet him. Don't you think God gives us the desires of our hearts? I mean, as long as our desires aren't sinful or anything, which yours sure don't seem to be. This world needs more Christian couples who are raising godly kids. What is that verse about delighting yourself in the Lord and He'll give you the desires of your heart?"

"But His timing isn't always the same as ours," Christy said. "And His way of doing things isn't always the same as ours."

"Yeah, God is weird," Katie said. "That's my philosophy. God is weird, and we are tweaked. He's full of surprises, and we make our lives harder than they need to be. It'd be great if everything always went the way we wanted it to, but it doesn't seem to be like that very often."

"You know what we should do, you guys?" Sierra suggested. "We should pray. Pray for ourselves and pray for our future husbands."

"I write letters to mine," Christy said, and then felt surprised at her own confession. She could feel the penetrating gaze of the other girls.

"What do you write to him?" Sierra asked.

"I don't know. What I'm feeling. Times when I'm thinking about what it will be like to be married to him, whoever he is. I tell him that I'm praying for him, and sometimes I write out my prayers. I've been writing to him for I guess about three years now."

"That is so cool," Sierra said.

"What do you do with the letters?" Tracy asked.

Christy smiled, feeling kind of silly to be revealing her little secret after all these years. "They're in a shoe box under my bed."

"I wish I'd kept my letter locked away," Tracy said almost inaudibly.

"What do you mean?" Christy asked.

"Nothing," Tracy said. "I think your idea is wonderful. I also think it's good to keep your letters a secret until the right time."

It was quiet for a minute, and then Sierra said, "Christy, can you imagine what it's going to be like on your wedding night?" She sniffed as if she might be crying. "Your future husband is going to feel like the most blessed guy in the whole world when you hand him that shoe box full of prayers and promises. What an incredible wedding present!"

Christy fell asleep dreaming of what it would be like to hand her shoe box full of letters to her future husband. She could see strong, manly hands eagerly receiving her gift. But in her dream, as she looked up, where the face of her future spouse should have been, there was only a big, fluffy cloud.

CHAPTER SEVEN

The Awesome Team

"You said last night that you wanted to talk?" Doug caught up with Christy and walked with her past the barren rose bushes on their way from the chapel to the castle. The early morning drizzle had turned into a sporadic sprinkling of white snowflakes that collected on Christy's eyelashes.

"It would be better if we had more time," Christy said, not sure what she wanted to say to him and not comfortable with the thought that anyone walking past them might hear.

"Our team meeting isn't for another five or ten minutes. We have training pretty much all afternoon. This is probably our best chance until after dinner. Why don't you tell me what you're thinking and feeling? I'd really like to hear."

Doug had switched into his counselor voice, and Christy wasn't sure she liked it. She wanted to talk to him as one friend to another, like a girlfriend would talk to her boyfriend. Not like a psycho patient to an all-wise counselor.

"Actually, it's nothing."

"Are you sure?"

"Yep, I'm sure." Christy forced a smile and blinked a fluttering snowflake from her eyelash. Everything was going so great for their team. The last thing she wanted was to cause division by questioning Doug on why he felt he wasn't honoring her. Or worse, to give in to the insecurities that arose in her last night when Sierra said she would never have guessed they were going together. Her confusion made her want to question Doug about his feelings for her. Her emotions kept chasing themselves around in a circle in her head. It would be best to try to stop her racing feelings long enough for their group to complete their outreach without disunity. She could always sit down with Doug back in California and spend as many hours as she needed to discuss their relationship and their future.

"You said yesterday that you wanted to go for a walk," Doug continued in his counselor voice. "Maybe we could squeeze one in this afternoon."

"Sure. That would be great." They could walk, but they wouldn't have to talk.

Doug and Christy now stood at the large front door of the castle. Christy noticed for the first time a brass lion-head door knocker with a brass ring in its mouth. At that moment, she felt as if she too held a brass ring between her teeth. Like that silent lion, she could hold on. He had apparently held on for centuries. She could hold on for a few weeks.

"Our team is meeting by the big windows in the drawing room," Doug said as he held the door open for Christy. "I'm going to see if I can borrow that guitar again. I'll meet you there."

Christy stopped at the "sweet trolley" as everyone called it, poured herself a cup of tea, and picked up a biscuit before reporting to the drawing room. All the other team members were taking their tea break and milling around the hallway. As Christy walked by, she noticed the variety of accents and the different ways the other students laughed and joked.

Katie stood in the corner with a guy Christy hadn't met yet. They seemed caught up in a serious discussion.

Katie noticed Christy and motioned for her to join them. "Christy, this is Jakobs. He's from Latvia. This is Christy."

Jakobs nodded his head in greeting and warmly shook Christy's hand.

"Jakobs is heading up the drama for the Amsterdam group. He's been giving me some great ideas."

Just then, Sierra, Stephen, and Tracy walked up, and Katie made introductions all around. A few minutes later, when they broke up into their team meetings, Katie grasped Christy by the arm and said, "Jakobs' grandfather spent twenty-five years in Siberia. Can you believe that? He was taken from his home and exiled because he was a pastor. I'm telling you, Christy, we have no clue what it means to be persecuted for our faith."

Katie's words were sobering. It seemed that in the past twenty-four hours she had gone from resisting any kind of cultural change to seeking as much input as she could from the variety of international students at the castle. That was Katie, though. Impulsive. Direct. And one who rarely looked back once she had put her mind to something new.

Exactly the opposite of me.

That realization didn't bother Christy, but it did make her admire Katie and inwardly wish she could be more flexible and open.

Christy penned those thoughts in her journal that night. She had retired to the dorm room early and was the only one there. The afternoon walk with Doug had never worked out. He didn't even sit by her at dinner. Right now he and Tracy were practicing their music, and the rest of her roommates were down in the drawing room, socializing for their last free hour before lights out.

Christy wanted to be alone to catch her breath. It was about this time only a week ago that she had been finishing up her packing for this trip and letting her imagination fill with expectations of all the amazing things she would experience. She had never expected the emotional confusion and stress the past week had brought.

Her diary had always served as a useful mirror, a place to put her feelings outside herself and then stand back and take a look. The examination nearly always changed her perspective. Tonight she wanted to do her examining without any roommates peeking over her shoulder. For a full fifteen minutes she had her wish. Then Avril, one of the English girls, came into the room crying.

"Are you okay?" Christy asked.

Avril was crying so much she couldn't answer. Christy put down her diary and went to Avril, opening her arms and offering her shoulder for Avril to cry on. She cried so hard Christy could feel the moist tears through her sweatshirt.

"I'm sorry," Avril said at last, sitting up and wiping her eyes with the back of her hand.

"That's okay," Christy said. "Is there anything I can do?"

"It's my brother. My mum just rang to tell me he's been in an automobile accident. I have to collect my things. Dr. Benson is driving me to the train station."

"Oh, Avril, that's awful! Is he okay?"

"He's still alive, but he's in critical condition." Avril's hands were shaking. "I don't know what to do first."

"Let me find you some tissue," Christy said, getting up and looking around the room. "Here you go. Now you just sit there and tell me where your suitcase is and which drawer is yours."

"It's under the bed. My drawer is the second one down."

Christy pulled out the blue suitcase and began to swiftly,

calmly transfer the clothes from the drawer into the suitcase. Avril fumbled for her bag hanging over the end of the bed and started to stuff her Bible, notebook, and other bedside items into it.

"Do you want me to get your shampoo and stuff from the bathroom?"

"Sure. Mine's the red striped bag with the broken zipper. You don't have to do all this, Christy."

"I don't mind," Christy said.

She found Avril's bag on the counter in the bathroom down the hall and tucked it into the suitcase. "Now what else? Your coat?"

"I have it already. I think that's all. I feel so awful about leaving." Avril stood and looped the bag over her shoulder while Christy snapped the clasps closed on the suitcase. "I hope I can come back in time to participate in the outreach."

"Don't feel bad," Christy said. She wanted to say something comforting. "God is kind of weird sometimes," she said, cautiously echoing Katie's words. "I'm sure it seems hard to understand why this is happening. I'm sorry it's happened. I promise I'll be praying for you and your brother."

"Thanks, Christy," Avril said, giving her a big hug and letting the next round of tears fall. "I'm so glad you were here for me. I'll be praying for you, too."

Avril pulled back and looked at Christy with an expression of fresh pain. "If I can't make it back, I don't know when I'll see you again. Maybe not until heaven."

Christy hugged her again, and in her ear she said, "Then I'll look forward to heaven even more than ever."

Now they were both crying. Without another word, Avril lifted her suitcase and walked across the room. She paused at the door and looked heavenward as if to say "Until then." Christy nodded, and Avril was gone.

That's when Christy fell apart. She threw herself onto her bed and let the tears fall. Tears for saying good-bye until heaven. Tears for the thought of how hard it would be if it were her own little brother who was in an accident. Tears earned over a week of trying hard to be strong, courageous, and understanding of everyone else's problems while her own insecurities had reached the breaking point.

"Did you hear about Avril's brother?" Katie said, bursting through the door. "Oh, I guess you did. Can you imagine how awful that would be? Yeah, I guess you can." Now Katie was crying too. "I can't believe I'm actually saying this, but I miss my family!"

Katie flopped on her own bed and cried out all her own tears while Christy released the rest of hers. A special bond formed as they let each other cry. Christy crawled into bed under her warm blankets and, with only a few more sobs, fell into a deep, exhausted sleep.

The next morning she stayed in bed, hoarsely telling a concerned Tracy that her throat hurt and she needed to sleep another hour or so. It was hard to go back to sleep while the other girls scurried around to get ready. Once they went to breakfast, Christy had no trouble nodding off.

She awoke sometime later. The room was empty. On a chair next to her bed sat a breakfast tray with a glass of orange juice, a pot of tea, white toast, and a tiny jar of orange marmalade. The note on top of the toast said, "Hope you feel better. Love, Tracy."

Christy propped herself up and poured a cup of tea. It was cold. The tray must have been there for quite some time. She drank the juice and crunched on the slice of toast before checking her alarm clock. It was 11:40. Almost time for lunch. Her throat no longer hurt. She felt rested and a little bit guilty about missing the morning meetings. However, she knew she had needed the sleep even more than she had realized. Part of her wanted to float back to dreamland, and another part of her felt she should get up and get going. The responsible side won.

"Christy, are you feeling better?" Sierra was the first one to notice her when she entered the dining room.

Doug noticed too. He got up from his seat, came across the room, and gave her a hug. "How are you doing?"

"I'm fine. It all caught up with me, I guess."

Katie now stood on her other side and said, "Jet lag finally got to you, huh? At least all you did was sleep instead of turn into a brat, like I did."

"I'm glad you're okay," Doug said. "Right after lunch all the people working with children are meeting in the conference room. Do you feel up to going?"

"Sure. I'm fine, really."

The lunch of chicken with some kind of cream sauce tasted bland, but Christy was hungry and gladly ate it all. She noticed then that nearly everything they ate had some kind of sauce or cream over the top of it. Whether it was meat or potatoes or even pie, it all came with cream.

She still felt a little spacey as the meeting for children's ministry started up. But soon she became excited about all the things the leaders were going over. They had adorable puppets available for the team members to use, a whole box of craft materials for each team, and helpful suggestions on how to get the kids to listen during the Bible story time. Christy looked over the handout of Bible stories and felt relieved that she knew them all and had even taught a couple of them to the toddlers at her home church.

At her team meeting later that afternoon, Christy gave a glowing report. "I could use one other person to help me with a puppet show. They gave us a script and everything. It seems pretty easy, and I think it would add a lot to our program this Saturday."

"I'll do it," Katie said. "Maybe we can work the puppets into the drama ministry somehow and get double use out of them."

"This is going to be awesome, you guys," Doug said enthusiastically. "How did your meeting go, Ian? Do you feel you'll be ready to preach it, brother?"

"Well, it's really a short talk more than a sermon, you know." Ian pushed up his wire-rimmed glasses. "I need to practice it in front of our group before Saturday."

"Right," Doug said. "That's what they told us in the leaders' meeting this afternoon. By Thursday everyone is supposed to present to us whatever his or her part of the program is. We'll start with the drama, then do the children's, the message, and then the music. Gernot, it would be great if you could help Christy with the children's program since you're rounding them up for soccer in order to get the kids there. Maybe she could take the little kids, and you could take the ones in grade school."

Gernot nodded.

"Especially the rowdy boys," Christy said. "You can have all of them."

"My specialty," Gernot said with a smile.

Christy found it hard to believe that this tall, slim guy would want to take on a bunch of hooligans.

She saw another side of Gernot that night after dinner, though. For their free time, the Belfast team challenged the Barcelona team to a game of Bible charades in the drawing room. Gernot had to act out Baalam and his talking donkey. Somehow he managed to play the angel, the donkey, and Baalam in lightning-fast time and without a word. They all laughed until their sides ached.

The charades turned out to be the best thing they could have done to relieve the tension of the week. Christy laughed and felt full of life, especially while she watched Doug act out Moses coming down from Mount Sinai with the Ten Commandments. It was like old times. He laughed, and after his performance, he sat next to Christy on the couch and put his arm around her. She felt as if everything was normal, the way life had been for the past few months of her life. Was she really half a world away, in England?

It was a good thing they slid the charades break in when they did, because the rest of the week was nonstop activities. Christy spent all of Wednesday working on her children's program. Katie practiced puppets with her for almost two hours, and then after lunch, Christy and Gernot went over the Bible story. They came up with some good ideas on how to work the puppet show into the middle of the story to make it more interesting and fun for the kids.

By Thursday morning, Christy felt ready and had everything together to practice her part of the program in front of the team. She felt excited, eager, and confident.

Katie, Sierra, and Stephen presented their drama to the group first, and it was amazing. The three of them worked well together, and the point of the drama was clear without being overdone.

"Any suggestions?" Doug asked after they had finished.

"Stephen, you had your back to the audience for a little bit at the beginning," Gernot pointed out. "It was hard to see what you were doing."

"Okay, I'll remember that."

"Anything else?"

"It was really good," Tracy said. "It got me right here," she said, patting her heart. "And I even knew ahead of time what you were going to do."

"It was great!" Christy agreed. She thought of how close the group now seemed and how well everyone was working together.

"Okay, Ian, you're on," Doug said.

When Ian stood in front of them, Christy learned how deceiving appearances could be. Ian looked so quiet and professor-like; yet when he stood before them and presented his message, they all sat still, absorbing every word. In less than fifteen minutes, he powerfully presented the Gospel and offered an invitation to anyone who wanted to know more. The team spontaneously began to clap when he finished.

"This is pretty exciting, you guys," Doug said. "Ian, that was perfect. Don't change a word. Now, do you all remember that we do the message last, and Ian will say if anyone wants to know more about God, they can stick around and talk to any of us."

Everyone nodded.

"Okay, your turn, Christy."

Suddenly she felt unprepared. Everyone else had done such a great job. What if she blew it? She fumbled for her notes, and then realized she had left them in the room because she had felt so confident. "Should we do the puppets first?"

"Sure," Doug said.

Katie joined Christy, and they plunged their hands into the puppets and began their play as practiced. It went okay. Everyone said it was great, and they laughed at all the appropriate times, but Christy felt so nervous, she wasn't even sure she had said all her lines. It did help break the ice for her story, though, and she sailed through that without losing her place. Instead of looking into the faces of her friends as she spoke, she tried to imagine the faces of little kids, and she felt more at ease.

"Good job," Doug praised her when she sat down. "Looks like we're on a roll here, team. Now for the music. I'd like to do one song with the whole group, and we can practice that tomorrow. Tracy and I have a song we'll do right before the message. Ready, Trace?"

Petite Tracy took her place standing next to Doug. He played an intro on the guitar, and they began to sing in perfect harmony. It was a song Tracy had written last summer about God never giving up on us and how He waits for us to invite Him to come in. Even though everyone else had done terrific jobs on their presentations, something about Doug and Tracy's singing was especially moving. They sounded so good together. The words to the song were so powerful. Christy held her breath as they held out the final note.

When they finished, there was a pause for several seconds before anyone responded. Clapping seemed almost irreverent. "That had to be the most beautiful song I've ever heard," Sierra said. "If I weren't already a Christian, I would be ready to make a commitment after that. Have you guys sung together a lot?"

"No," Tracy said, her cheeks flushing.

Doug put his arm around her and gave her one of his hugs. "What did I tell you?" he said. "We're an awesome team."

That night while she was trying to fall asleep Christy ran that scene over and over in her mind. Was Doug saying the whole team was awesome? Then why was he looking at Tracy and hugging her when he said it?

Christy couldn't sing, at least not like Tracy. Sometimes Christy and Doug had sung together in the car for fun, but her voice never sounded the way Tracy's did with Doug's.

Then, like a huge wave breaking over her and pulling her under with its force, Christy felt furious with Tracy. She wanted to reach over the few feet to Tracy's bed, shake her awake, and yell at her that she had no right being so close to Doug. Christy was too mad to cry. And too hurt to think clearly. How could Tracy do this to her?

Do what? All Tracy and Doug did was sing together. Tracy didn't do anything wrong. What am I thinking?

Christy rolled over and fought against what she already knew to be true. A still, small voice was speaking to her. She had heard it before. Once, in high school she had heard it when she knew she should give up her place on the cheerleading squad. And once again she had heard it at San Clemente beach when she gave back her ID bracelet to Todd. Both times the voice told her those were the actions she should take. Now she wrapped her pillow around her ears, as if that would make the voice go away.

"Forget it, God," she muttered under her breath. Then she cried bitter, salty tears while murmuring, "I'm sorry. I really don't hate Tracy. I'm sorry."

That was enough to help relieve her hurt and allow her a night of fitful sleep. Her subconscious told her the tears weren't over her anger at Tracy. They were long-ago tears over losing Todd, and they were frightened tears over the thought that she might be about to lose Doug. Then where would she be? There was no one else.

CHAPTER EIGHT

Sir Honesty

Christy avoided talking to anyone the next morning, especially Tracy. It wasn't hard, because all the girls in their room overslept, and they all frantically scrambled to make it to breakfast in time. It was the last day before their local outreach, and all of them had much to do to get ready.

Christy sat next to Sierra at breakfast and across from Doug. It was a relief to her when Tracy entered the dining room and sat at another table without making eye contact with any of them.

They had an hour after breakfast for personal quiet time and devotions, which Christy spent scribbling postcards to her family. She wrote surface information, trying to sound cheery and as if everything were going wonderfully. She then gathered her children's materials and made sure she was the first one to their team meeting. The others showed up a few minutes later. Everyone except Tracy.

Doug asked Stephen to open their meeting in prayer. Doug looked unusually solemn and cleared his throat several times before starting the meeting. "I have something to announce," he said.

Christy felt her heart start to pound.

"Tracy has asked to be on another team." Doug just laid out the information without explanation or personal comment.

Christy was shocked. She hadn't said a thing to Tracy. She had asked God last night to forgive her for her anger, and she had made sure she didn't do anything out of the ordinary to give Tracy the impression Christy had ever been mad at her. It couldn't be Christy's fault.

"What's wrong?" Gernot asked. "Why does she want to switch teams?"

Doug shrugged. "All I know is that she does."

"Do we have to meet right now?" Sierra asked. "Could we all take a little break and get back together after lunch?"

"That's a good idea," Ian agreed.

"Okay," Doug said, "we'll meet here right after lunch."

They all went their separate ways, except for Christy and Doug. Doug sat with his head down, and Christy wasn't sure he knew she was standing there.

"Maybe we should go for that walk now," Doug said to her without looking up.

"Sure," she said timidly. Was he mad? Hurt? She couldn't tell.

Christy grabbed her umbrella, pulled on her jacket, and waited for Doug to rise. She felt sick inside. Tracy must be leaving because of her. That was the only explanation she could think of. Obviously something powerful was going on between Tracy and Doug. Christy knew Tracy would rather take all the responsibility and sacrifice on herself than cause conflict for anyone else.

Doug silently walked with Christy through the castle, out the front door, and around to the meadow. He remained silent until they were all the way to the stone bridge that spanned the brook and connected the meadow with the forest.

Christy struggled with what to say, what to think, what to feel.

She wanted Doug to be the first one to speak. He remained silent.

They stopped on the stone bridge. Doug tossed a pebble into the white, foaming water below.

"I haven't been fair to you, Christy," he finally said. No other words followed.

Christy wasn't sure what to think. "What do you mean, Doug?"

It took him a few minutes before he asked, "Did Tracy ever tell you why we broke up?"

"No."

"It was because of a letter she wrote me. Actually, it was a poem."

Christy remembered Tracy's comment a few nights earlier about how it was a good idea Christy had kept all her shoe box letters a secret. Now it was beginning to make sense. Tracy must have liked Doug more than he liked her, and she had revealed her feelings in a letter.

"You see," Doug continued, "that was three years ago, and I wasn't ready to get serious about anyone. Plus, I had this thing about you."

"This 'thing'?" Christy questioned.

"I hope you'll take this the right way, Christy." Doug looked like a little boy. "When something is unattainable, sometimes that makes a guy want it so much that he thinks he can't rest until he conquers it. Does that make sense?"

"You're saying I was unattainable?"

"Yes, in a way. For so long you were only interested in Todd, and the more I watched you guys, the more I thought I'd be better for you than he was. I don't want to hurt your feelings by saying all this, Christy."

Christy drew in a long breath of brisk air through her nostrils and squarely faced Doug. "You don't have to say anything else, Doug. I understand, and I agree with you. We should break up."

"Break up? It sounds so harsh when you say it that way," Doug said. "That's not what I'm trying to say."

"Look," Christy said calmly, "you and I have been good friends for a long time. We should have known that it would be best to stay friends instead of trying to make something more out of it."

"That's my fault," Doug said. "All last summer you were right when you wouldn't agree to go together. I was stubborn. Trying to prove something to myself, I guess. I'm sorry, Christy."

"I don't think you should be sorry, Doug. I mean, when you think about it, even when we started going together, we still acted the same—like we were good friends. I admire you for not kissing me. It makes it easier now to break up."

Doug shook his head. "I don't like saying that we're breaking up."

"Then what are we doing?"

"I don't know. What *were* we doing? I mean, why did I wait so long and pressure you so much to go out with me? I've been a jerk."

"No, you haven't. That's not the way I see it, Doug. I think both of us had to test our relationship and see if there was anything more to it. There wasn't. We're good friends. You're free, Doug. You don't owe me anything. Not even an apology. I admire you, I appreciate you, and I think you're a great guy."

"And I think you're an incredible woman, Christy. That's the problem. I've always admired you, and I've wondered for so long if maybe there might be something more. You know, fireworks."

Christy pressed her lips together and looked down into the water rushing beneath the bridge. She had to admit she liked

Doug, but he had never given her goose bumps. It was humbling to know she apparently had never given him goose bumps either. Still, the honesty helped. A lot. Their feelings were mutual. It was too bad they hadn't been able to confess that to each other earlier.

"I feel as if we're in junior high," Christy said.

"I think when it comes to gut-level emotions," Doug said, "we tend to express them the most accurately and honestly when we're in junior high. As we get older, we only think we're sophisticated because we learn to play some complicated games. I'm sorry I've played this one so long with you, Christy. I never meant to hurt you."

"I know," Christy said, feeling hot tears well up in her eyes. "And as long as we're being so honest, I need to tell you that I've played the game too. It was much easier to keep things the way they were than to let you go, because then I wouldn't have anybody."

Doug, the tenderhearted counselor, put his arm around her and said, "You'll always have me as your friend, Christy. And now as your new, improved, completely honest friend, I feel I can honor you. And you can honor me."

Christy stood for a long moment with her head resting on Doug's shoulder, gazing through misty eyes at the meadow beyond the creek. She recognized it as the same meadow she and Tracy had looked out on from their window seat. This was the meadow Christy had imagined a knight in shining armor riding through on his trusty steed, ready to storm the castle and take his princess. Now here she stood, shivering on this old bridge, letting go of her pretend knight.

"Kneel," she suddenly said, turning toward Doug and startling him. "Kneel!"

He slowly obliged, giving her a confused look as he went down beside her on one knee.

"I knight thee Sir Douglas, the Honest," Christy said, gently tapping him on each shoulder with her closed umbrella. "Arise, fair friend. I believe a true princess awaits you in the castle."

Doug looked up. No words passed between them, only smiles of admiration exchanged by two close friends.

"You ready to go back?" Doug asked, rising to his feet.

"Actually, I think I'd like to be by myself for a while. Why don't you go on back? You and Tracy have some honesty to catch up on."

Doug took off jogging across the meadow. Christy smiled, thinking how this knight didn't even need a white horse.

As she stood listening to the gurgling brook and the far-off, high-pitched twitter of a lone bird in the forest, she felt a rush of contentment. She had done the right thing. There were no more confused, hidden feelings for her to keep buried in her heart. Doug and Tracy were suited for each other and the kind of couple God could use to further His kingdom here on earth.

Then, from out of nowhere, came an overwhelming sense of loss. She had nobody. Katie was right the other night when she told Sierra that Christy had always had a guy in her life. Even when she broke up with Todd, Fred was there, paying attention to her the next day. It didn't matter that she didn't like Fred. What mattered was that for more than four years she had had some guy in her life. Now there was no one. No one she was interested in, and no one interested in her. The hole inside felt bottomless.

It began to drizzle. Christy hid under her umbrella and stomped her feet to warm them up. She felt really cold now, chilled inside and out. Not even a cup of tea would make a difference.

The dismal forest on the other side of the bridge beckoned her to run to it and hide herself among the brambles. She could stay there for days, and no one would ever know.

The intense, cold tingles in her feet made her snap out of her dramatic plotting and walk back to the castle. Thin clouds now hung over the highest of the castle's turrets. It looked cold and gloomy. Just like she felt inside.

When she reached the front door, she spotted the brass lion head. The ring still hung between his clenched teeth. Maybe she was glad she no longer had to hold on to her circle of feelings for Doug. Maybe she was free now.

Free for what? Free to meet another guy? Free to go on without a guy in my life? What if there's nobody? Ever! What if I never have another boyfriend in my life and I die an old maid?

Christy gave the lion a sympathetic pat on the nose and shook out her wet umbrella before entering. The smell of lunch greeted her, and she slipped quietly into the dining room, where most of the students had nearly finished the meal.

"Could you pass the tea, please?" She sat in the first open spot she saw, which was right by the door. Doug had his back to her, three tables away, and Tracy was sitting next to him. Christy assumed the two of them had talked. Everything between them would be settled now, and their relationship could move forward. Their team would have its unity back. Everything would be great. Just great.

Christy took a sip of tea and quickly put down her cup. It was lukewarm and too strong. "Excuse me," she said, pushing back her chair.

She left the dining room as quickly as her appetite had left her. Rushing up the stairs, she retreated to the stillness of the dorm room, where she changed her clothes, starting with her damp socks. Being dry and semi-warm helped.

As she was lacing up her boots, Sierra walked in and looked surprised to see her. "There you are! I wondered what happened to you. Did you get any lunch?"

"I wasn't very hungry. I went for a walk down to the creek and got really cold. All I wanted to do was put on some dry clothes."

"Doug canceled our afternoon team meeting. We're supposed to pack up our stuff so we'll be ready to leave at 6:30 in the morning. I'm thinking a nap sounds pretty good."

Christy nodded. "A nap does sound good."

"Oh, and did you hear?" Sierra said, pulling off her shoes and sticking her feet under the blankets on her bed. "Tracy is back on the team. I don't know what the problem was. At lunch, Doug said she changed her mind and was going to stay with our team. That's all he said, and she just sat there smiling. I tell you, Christy, it's a soap opera around here."

"I broke up with Doug," Christy blurted out. "Or actually, we both agreed to break up and go back to being just friends."

"You're kidding! Oh, Christy! I'm sorry. I didn't know."

"He and Tracy belong together," Christy said.

Sierra looked at Christy with admiration on her freckled face. "You have to be the most noble person I've ever met. After all Katie told me the other night, and now here you go and break up with him so he and Tracy can get back together . . ." Sierra paused as the door to their room opened and Tracy and Katie came in.

"I was right," Katie said, her red hair swishing as she turned her head from Christy to Tracy and back to Christy. "I told you she would be hibernating under those covers. That's what I have on my schedule this afternoon."

Tracy walked over to her bed and sat on the edge, facing Christy. Her heart-shaped face looked so delicate. "Mrs. Bates from the kitchen is going into town today. I asked her if you and I could ride with her. There's a little restaurant I heard about, and I thought maybe we could go for tea and have a chance to talk."

Christy was aware of Sierra and Katie's listening ears, even though they pretended to be looking at something on Sierra's bed.

Perhaps it would be better if they went somewhere to talk. "Sure," Christy said. "What time?"

"First I have to meet with some of the people doing music for the other teams. How about if you and I meet Mrs. Bates down in the kitchen at 2:30?"

"Okay, I'll be there."

Tracy grabbed a notebook at the end of her bed and left for her meeting.

"Are you all right?" Katie asked, turning her attention to Christy.

Christy let out a huge sigh. "I feel like a dork. A total dork. Why did I ever start going with Doug? It was so pointless."

"Do you want to join our club?" Sierra asked. "Katie and I are going to start a club called the P.O. Box."

"Right," Katie said with a glimmer in her bright green eyes. "It stands for 'pals only,' and the 'box' is for the shoe boxes we're going to start filling with letters."

Christy smiled and shook her head. "You guys are hilarious."

"So, what do you think?" Sierra said. "Guys are not worth all this grief. It's pals only for us." She and Katie slapped a high five. "P.O." said Sierra.

"Right-o," answered Katie. "P.O. rules forever!"

Christy lifted her right hand into the air. Katie slapped her a high five.

Sierra galloped across the room and did the same. With a whoop, she said, "Member number three! All right, P.O. forever!"

Christy had to laugh. "You guys, it sounds like you're saying 'B.O.' like you want to have body odor forever."

Katie started to crack up. "That's it," she said. "That's our secret weapon to keep the guys away. B.O. forever!"

CHAPTER NINE

Garden of the Heart

The first thing Christy noticed when she and Tracy scrambled into Mrs. Bates' car was that the steering wheel was on the "wrong" side. She hadn't noticed it so much in the car that had picked them up at the train station the first night, because she was riding in the backseat. Now it felt awkward since she was sitting in the front, in the passenger seat, which was actually where she sat to drive her car at home.

It was even a stranger sensation riding down the narrow country lane on the wrong side of the road, with fast, little cars passing them on the wrong side.

"This is a beautiful drive," Tracy said. "Thanks for taking us."

"Not at all," Mrs. Bates replied. "I'll give you a lift to the tea shop, and then, if it would be agreeable with you, I'll come round to collect you at half-four."

Christy realized she must mean 4:30 and the "coming round to collect" must mean picking them up.

"That would be fine. Thank you," Tracy said.

They continued down the lane, under a bridge, around a winding curve with a moss-covered stone wall, and past two men wearing long black boots, dark jackets, and black riding hats, seated on very tall horses.

For Christy, there was no mistaking where they were. This was exactly how she had always pictured the English countryside. Her only wish was that she could return in the spring, or maybe even in the summer, when the green meadows would be polka-dotted with white lambs and the trees clothed in their proper, leafy attire. It must be absolutely beautiful then.

Once in town, Mrs. Bates edged the car into a narrow wedge of a parking space so the girls could climb out. They stood in front of a quaint building called "The Cheery Kettle Tea Shoppe."

"Half-four, then?" Mrs. Bates said.

"Yes, we'll see you then," Tracy said and waved good-bye.

A bell above the door rang merrily as they stepped into the restaurant. Soothing classical music floated through the air. Five or six round tables stood in the small room, with a vase of bright flowers and a white lace tablecloth atop each of them. Along the walls were lots of pictures and knickknacks. A bookshelf with an ornate rail ran along the top of the wall near the ceiling. The rack held clumps of old books, china plates, and photographs in pewter frames. In the corner stood a majestic grandfather clock that bonged three times as they sat down.

For a minute Christy forgot they had come here for a heart-to-heart talk. She felt intrigued and delighted by the charm of this place.

"Don't you love this?" she asked Tracy. Christy whispered because it seemed everything was hushed and calm around them.

"It's so quaint," Tracy agreed.

A round woman in a blue apron came up to their table just as two older women wearing hats came into the tea room and seated themselves at a table across the room.

"We'd like some tea," Tracy said, ordering for both of them.

"And a nice sweet for you today, miss?" the woman asked. She looked like Mrs. Rosey-Posey, a character from one of Christy's favorite children's books. Christy half expected the woman to offer them some chocolate covered cherries like in one of Mrs. Rosey-Posey's stories. Instead, she offered fresh apple pie or raisin scones.

"I'll have the scones," Christy said. She wasn't exactly sure what they were, but they sounded much more British than apple pie.

"Me too," Tracy agreed.

"Cream for both of you?" the woman asked.

Christy thought she meant cream for the tea and answered yes. The cream turned out to be a small bowl of whipped cream that came with the scones. "What do we do with the whipped cream?" Christy whispered after the woman walked away.

"I guess put it on these. They look like English muffins only flakier, like a biscuit." Tracy broke open her scone and scooped some whipped cream on top. "Oh, this is good!"

Christy prepared her tea the way she liked it, with milk and sugar, and then followed Tracy's lead, putting the whipped cream on the scone. It was yummy. Christy couldn't help but feel like a little girl who was playing dress-up in her mother's clothes and having a tea party. She wondered if Tracy felt the same way.

"I'm glad we could come here," Tracy said. "This is a nice, quiet place for us to talk."

Christy nodded, licking a dab of whipped cream off her top lip and wondering if she should bring up the topic of Doug first. She wasn't quite sure what to say. Tracy obviously knew they were no longer "together" and that he was free to pursue his relationship with Tracy. There wasn't a whole lot to talk about.

"Did Doug tell you why we broke up before?" Tracy asked.

"He told me today you wrote a letter, but he wasn't ready to be serious about anyone. I remembered what you said the other night in the room, and figured you put your heart out on paper, and he rejected it."

"I didn't feel like he was rejecting it," Tracy said cautiously. "He just pulled back. Big time. And then we decided to break up. It was mutual, but we never talked about what I wrote to him."

Tracy took a sip of tea and continued. "You know how Todd was always saying the guy should be the initiator and the girl should be the responder? Well, that's sort of what the problem was. I wrote Doug this poem, and I was initiating way too much. For the past three years I've hung back, wondering if I'd ever get another chance to respond and not initiate."

Christy thought of what Katie had said about Doug: His love was patient. If Doug had been patient, Tracy had been even more so. Obviously Doug had meant a lot to her for a long time, but Tracy had kept it all inside, waiting. What Christy admired most was that Tracy had never shown one speck of jealousy toward Christy while she and Doug were together.

"What I want to know, Christy, if you feel comfortable telling me, is why you broke up with Doug."

"I have a question for you first," Christy said. "Why did you ask to be put on another team?"

Tears began to fill Tracy's gentle eyes. "After Doug and I sang together last night, I knew I couldn't handle it any longer. I couldn't be around him and keep my feelings bottled up. You see, a couple of times on this trip Doug and I have been alone. Like when we were practicing. He said some things that were nicer than the average Doug-type of things, and I got the impression he felt more for me than he had ever let on."

Suddenly Christy felt betrayed. Doug had been two-timing her. Her expression must have reflected her indignation because Tracy said, "He never said anything obvious or anything against you. It was mostly a feeling that maybe he liked me. It felt complicated, and I didn't want to hurt you in any way, Christy, or hurt Doug or myself, for that matter. I thought the easiest thing would be to walk away."

"I was the one who needed to walk away, not you," Christy said. "And to answer your question of why I broke up with him, it was because it had become evident to me, well . . . to both of us, really, that our relationship was never going to grow beyond the level of good friends. It was kind of silly to even say we were going together since neither of us felt or acted that way. I realized that the other night when Sierra was so surprised we were going together. We weren't being completely honest with each other. Neither of us felt like we were going together inwardly, and neither of us acted like it outwardly."

Tracy wrapped her hands around her china teacup as if to warm them. Then, looking up at Christy, she said, "Are you sure? Very, very sure?"

"Absolutely. I think you two belong together. I can't believe it's taken this long for all of us to figure it out."

Tracy smiled. "I can't tell you how happy I feel right now. When Doug came up to me before lunch, I was by the rose bushes, walking back from the chapel. He came running across the green, calling my name. I'll never forget the look on his face. He told me about your talk and how you dubbed him Sir Honesty, and then he asked if I was ready to unlock the garden gate because this time he was ready to come in." Tracy looked starry-eyed.

"Did he mean the rose garden? There's no gate there," Christy said.

"No, you see, he was remembering the poem I had sent him three years ago."

"A poem?" Christy asked.

"Yes, that's what the letter was. Do you want to hear it?"

"You have it memorized?" Christy poured another cup of tea for each of them from the stout silver pot.

"I think I do. Let me try and see how far I get.

> Within my heart a garden grows,
> wild with violets and fragrant rose.
> Bright daffodils line the narrow path,
> my footsteps silent as I pass.
> Sweet tulips nod their heads in rest;
> I kneel in prayer to seek God's best.
> For 'round my garden a fence stands firm
> to guard my heart so I can learn
> who should enter, and who should wait
> on the other side of my locked gate.
> I clasp the key around my neck
> and wonder if the time is yet.
> If I unlocked the gate today,
> would you come in? Or run away?"

Christy sat mesmerized by Tracy's words. "You wrote that?"

Tracy nodded. "Kind of bold, huh?"

"I think it's beautiful," Christy said.

"Well, when I gave it to Doug three years ago, I guess I freaked him out. He ran away. He remembered it, though," Tracy said, the dreamy look returning. "That's why today he said if I unlocked the garden gate this time, he would come in."

Christy sipped at her hot tea and pondered Tracy's words. "This is so hopelessly romantic, I can't believe it. Why did you let me stand between you all this time? I had no idea!"

Tracy leaned forward. "If I had told you about my feelings for Doug, you would have pulled back and never dated him."

"That would have been okay," Christy said.

Tracy shook her head. "No, don't you see? It had to follow its natural course. Doug had to decide for himself if there was anything between the two of you. You had to see if there was anything there. Doug is so pure-hearted and sincere. It wasn't hard to wait. Well, up until last night it wasn't hard. Then after we sang together, I thought I was going to burst!"

The two friends sat sipping the remainder of their tea, pondering the events of the past few days, months, and years. "Katie is right," Christy said. "God is so weird. His way of doing things is bizarre."

A smile crept across Tracy's face. "And I wouldn't want God to be any other way."

"Will you promise me one thing?" Christy asked.

"Sure. What?"

"If, or should I say when, you and Doug get married, can I be a bridesmaid? I want a front-row view of when he kisses you for the first time."

Tracy let a nervous bubble of laughter explode a little too loudly, and the older women across the room gave them a look of mild disapproval. Tracy quickly drew her white linen napkin up to her mouth to muffle her chuckle.

"You really are a true friend, Christy. And if we ever do get married, yes, of course I'd love to have you stand with me as one of my bridesmaids. As long as you promise me that I can be a bridesmaid at your wedding too."

All Christy's feelings of contentment and awe drained from her. Christy couldn't imagine herself ever letting her feelings grow for another guy again. But she could picture herself standing at the gate of her heart's garden, making sure the gate was locked tight. She felt like swallowing the key.

"Hallo, girls!" Mrs. Bates' cheerful voice called out from behind them.

"Oh, is it time to go already?" Christy asked, glancing at the grandfather clock in the corner. "I hope we haven't kept you waiting."

"Not at all. I have to arrange a few things in the boot, so I'll meet you at the car when you're ready."

Tracy and Christy figured out how much they owed for their lovely tea and paid at the cash register. Out front they noticed Mrs. Bates was busily rearranging a variety of boxes and parcels like a jigsaw puzzle in the car's trunk.

"Do you need some help?" Tracy asked.

"These bundles won't quite fit here in the boot."

"The boot?" Christy asked. "You mean the trunk? I thought you were talking about the boots on your feet."

Mrs. Bates looked up. "No, the boot. This is the boot. The front of the car is the bonnet. Why? What do you call it?"

"The trunk and the hood."

With a ripple of laughter, Mrs. Bates said, "Well then, I can't seem to fit these things in the trunk."

"I can hold some things on my lap in the backseat," Tracy volunteered.

"Actually, it's my turn to sit in the back," Christy said. "I'll hold them."

"Brilliant!" Mrs. Bates shut the trunk, or rather, the boot, and handed several packages to Christy for her to balance on her lap once she wedged herself into the already half loaded backseat.

They drove down the country lane, with Mrs. Bates and Tracy chattering all the way. Christy kept silent in the backseat beneath her packages. She felt this was where she belonged, taking a backseat to Tracy, who for years had taken a backseat to her. It was a humbling experience.

At the castle Christy and Tracy hurried to prepare everything for their early morning departure to Noelsbury.

"Should we pack a change of clothes?" Christy asked.

"We're supposed to be back here tomorrow night," Tracy said. "I think all we need is a jacket and our materials for the outreach."

"I don't know how to pack these huge puppets and all these craft materials," Christy said. Then she had an idea. She forced everything into her suitcase and zipped it shut. With the pullout handle and wheels, she was sure it would be easy to get on and off the train.

"Brilliant!" Tracy said, eyeing the suitcase.

" 'Brilliant,' " Christy repeated. "Isn't that the funniest word? Everyone around here says it. We better watch out, or before we know it, Doug will be replacing his 'awesome' with 'brilliant.' "

Tracy sat on the edge of her bed and pulled a brush through her hair, checking her reflection in a small oval mirror she held in her hand. Christy thought how pretty Tracy was, how sweet and kind and perfect for Doug in every way.

Christy's talk with Doug on the bridge seemed a decade ago. So much had changed in her feelings after the talk and after she understood about the garden in Tracy's heart.

However, one thing hadn't changed—the deep, hollow ache right in the middle of her stomach. The ache of loneliness.

CHAPTER TEN

The True Princess

"It *would* be pouring rain," Christy muttered. She stood inside the small train station with her other teammates, waiting for their host pastor to arrive and drive them to the church for their Saturday outreach. The train ride had taken a little more than two hours, and although it was almost nine in the morning, it still felt like the middle of the night.

A bright red minivan pulled up in the parking lot, and a man in a black raincoat got out and ran inside. "You're here!" he said when he spotted the group. "Sorry to keep you waiting. I'm Reverend Allistar."

Doug shook hands with him and introduced everyone.

"Shall we go then?" the pastor said, opening the door to the pouring rain.

"Let me get that for you, Christy," Doug said, offering to carry her suitcase with all the puppets and craft materials tucked neatly inside. He smiled, and she thanked him. It all seemed so normal again, so natural for the two of them to be friends. It also had seemed natural to see Tracy sitting next to him during the train ride this morning and for Doug to have his arm resting across the back of her seat as he listened to her with interest.

The team had to squeeze to fit inside the minivan. Christy was glad the drive to the church was only fifteen minutes. They all tumbled out in the rain when they arrived. Gernot handed Christy's suitcase to her once they were inside the small, stone church and said, "I'll help you with the children since they might not be too keen on soccer in the rain."

"Brilliant!" said Doug, who had overheard Christy and Gernot talking.

Tracy and Christy burst out laughing. "We were afraid this might happen," Tracy said. "You're changing into a 'brilliant' man!"

Doug looked deeply into Tracy's eyes. The two of them seemed to exchange some unspoken message. Christy felt a bit uncomfortable.

"Actually, you've always been a brilliant man," Tracy said.

Doug loved receiving praise. He used to smile whenever Christy complimented him. Now Tracy's words made him glow.

"Where would you like us to set up for the children?" Christy asked the pastor, moving away from Doug and Tracy.

"This way," he said, leading Christy and Gernot down the short hallway to a large, carpeted room. "Please feel free to arrange the room to your liking."

Gernot began to move chairs, creating a clever stage for their puppet show. Christy unzipped her suitcase and lifted out the craft materials. From that moment on, she barely stopped moving all day.

Their first group of children arrived with bountiful energy. Christy and Gernot's job was to keep the young ones occupied while their parents were in the sanctuary meeting. Since it was a small church, Christy wondered if the noisy children could be heard down the hallway. But all in all, the morning program went smoothly. She was glad they had enough crafts to keep the older kids interested and that all of them liked the puppet show.

Gernot saved the day during the last fifteen minutes when the children began to get hungry and tired. He seemed to know an endless number of indoor games, which the children loved.

After their morning session, a cold lunch was served to them in the church kitchen. Doug asked Christy how it went with the children.

"Fine," she said, "thanks to Gernot. We could use some more help in there, though. If anyone else would like to come in during the afternoon program, that would be great."

The next session began at 1:30, and a new flock of kids arrived. There weren't so many at first. Christy thought it might be easier than the morning bunch. Then a few more children arrived, and then a few more, and pretty soon the noise level in the room rose. They decided to move right into the Bible story and the puppet show to see if they could get all the kids to sit down and, hopefully, to quiet down. It seemed to work.

Halfway through the puppet show, Tracy and Sierra entered the room and stood in the back.

"Ian is giving his message first this time," Tracy explained after the puppet show as they gathered the children in groups of five to work on their craft. "So we have some time before we do the drama and music. How can we help out here?"

"We're making paper crowns," Christy said. "These stars don't seem to peel off very easily. You could help with that. And if one of you wants to pass out the crayons, that would be great. The littler kids usually break the crayons, so give them the fat colors or the ones that are already broken."

"You're quite the natural children's ministry woman," Katie said. Then, striking a pose with her arms muscled out like a weight lifter, she added in a low, beefy voice, "I am ministry woman." She flexed her arm muscles again, and Christy laughed. Some of the children noticed Katie's muscle-bound pose and laughed at her too.

"Would you kids like to hear a little song?" Tracy asked. She sat down in a circle of girls busily maneuvering their blunt scissors around the edges of their cut-out paper crowns. With her high, charming voice, Tracy sang a song about a baby bird in its nest and how it trusted its heavenly Father and we should too.

"Sing another!" the children asked.

Tracy sang about how the mountains, the meadows, and even the trees sing out their praise to God, and we should too. Christy was pretty sure these were all songs Tracy had written. She could picture Tracy singing them one day with Doug.

Katie whispered to Christy, "I am song woman." She struck another muscle-flexing pose.

"And what are you, Katie?"

"I am drama woman," she said, readjusting her pose so she could check her watch. "And I must go." She motioned to Sierra, who was sitting on the floor helping a small girl affix her stars in just the right place on her crown.

Sierra hopped up, and on her way to join Katie, she whispered to Christy, "I'll be back. This is fun!"

Tracy left too. As soon as the crowns were finished, the children brought them to Christy so she could measure their head size and staple the crowns in the back.

When the parents came to pick up the kids, one little boy put his crown on his head and cried out, "Mummy, Mummy, look! Jesus is the King of everything!"

The "mummy" smiled and said to Christy, "Thanks so much. I really enjoyed the program. It gave me a lot to think about."

"And Mummy," the boy continued, "Jesus loves me."

Christy felt good knowing that the message had come across clearly for the little guy. She wished his mom didn't look quite so serious and unsure.

"I have something for you," Christy said. She reached in her craft box and pulled out one of the booklets the ministry team was giving to people who said they wanted to know more about Christ. "Here. Maybe this will help you to think through what you've heard. We'll be back tonight at six o'clock it you would like to come again."

She didn't know if she sounded too pushy. The program would be the same as this afternoon, so why would the lady want to come again? Still, Christy was glad she hadn't let the woman walk away empty-handed.

The last child had just left when Doug popped his head in the door and said, "Grab your coats! We're ready to go. You can leave all this."

Christy and Gernot were the last to squeeze into the minivan. The pastor drove fast down the narrow streets of the town to their appointed location at the town square for their four o'clock drama presentation. Christy felt relieved that she didn't have any responsibilities for this portion so she could catch her breath.

The drama team went to work in the van, applying make-up and a few simple costume pieces. Doug and Ian carried the props out to the center of the square and tried to find the driest spot to set up. The good news was that the rain had stopped. The bad news was that the cobblestone square was wet and slippery and only a few people were out and about.

Still, the team stayed on course, and right at four o'clock the drama team began their performance before a gathering of seven local people. A few other people joined them, and by about halfway through the presentation, Christy noticed the crowd had swelled to about thirty.

"Here," Doug whispered to Christy near the end of the play. "Be ready to pass these out." He handed her a bunch of booklets explaining how to become a Christian and another handful of flyers announcing their evening meeting at the church.

As soon as the drama ended, the crowd spontaneously applauded, which Christy thought was a good sign. Several teenagers and older children were in the crowd. Christy went right up to them and offered a brochure before they walked away.

"Where are you from?" a young teenage boy asked her.

"Some of us are from America, some from Germany. We're part of an outreach team," Christy explained.

"Why are you here?"

Before Christy had time to think through her answer, she said, "Because people need Jesus, and we want to tell them about Him."

The boy snickered and walked away. Christy felt foolish. The other people she handed brochures to were polite and thanked her. She wished she hadn't blown it with that boy, though.

To her surprise, the boy showed up at their six o'clock meeting. There were a lot of teenagers, and Reverend Allistar said many of the people were from his congregation. Christy and Gernot had their hands full with more than forty-five children. Tracy, Sierra, and Katie came in later to help out, which was a good thing, because when Christy gave the lesson and told the children how they could become Christians, thirteen of them raised their hands. Gernot and the other team members went right to work, counseling the children while Christy started the craft for the others.

"It was amazing," Christy said when their team scrunched

back in the minivan so the pastor could drive them to the station. "The lesson, the invitation, everything was the same as the two earlier meetings, yet this time thirteen kids responded. Why?"

"That's part of what they told us in training," Doug said. "Our job is to be faithful to present the message of salvation through Christ and then trust God for the results. His Spirit moves sometimes when we're not looking. Altogether in the meetings today, we had eighteen people who wanted more information and four people who prayed with us to give their lives to Christ."

"Did you give me that list of addresses?" Reverend Allistar called over his shoulder as he drove.

"Yes," said Doug, "I think you put it in your office on your desk."

"Right," the pastor responded. He parked the car and turned around with a look of delight on his face. "You have done so much today in helping me to further the ministry in this town. Thank you, thank you."

They each shook hands with him in turn after they got out of the van. Christy felt as if they had really done so little. She had had fun, actually. It was a bit wild at times, but all in all, she thought it had been easy and fun.

As soon as they were on the train, Christy turned to Sierra, who was seated next to her, and asked, "Do you know who the four people were who made commitments to Christ? Was one of them a teenage guy who was at the drama this afternoon?"

"No, they were all women," Sierra said.

Christy silently prayed for the mystery guy and for the children who had said they wanted to be Christians. About twenty minutes into the train ride, when everyone else was involved in a conversation or asleep, Sierra asked Christy, "Do you think you could do this all the time?"

"What, you mean work with kids?"

"Yes, and do outreach work like this."

Christy thought a moment and said, "You know, I think I could. Maybe I've found my niche."

"You did seem quite natural in there," Sierra agreed.

Christy struck a muscle-man pose the way Katie had earlier and said, "I am children's ministry woman."

Sierra laughed. "I don't know what I am yet. I like the drama and everything, but I don't know if that's my strongest point."

"What else do you like to do?" Christy asked.

"I like to write and make up stories."

"Maybe you should be a writer," Christy suggested.

"You know, I was thinking about writing a story about a princess and how she was looked down on because she wasn't very good-looking. Actually, she was ugly. She gets locked outside the castle, and the peasants are all mean to her. Then one person shows kindness to her, and in the end they find out she's a princess, and she rewards the person. What do you think?"

"I like it," Christy said. "You should write it. This sure is the place for inspiration, isn't it? I've been dreaming about knights and princesses while we've been at Carnforth Hall too."

"It's also the place for thinking about marriage," Sierra said. "This P.O. Box stuff is getting harder the more I watch other people pair up. You know, I'm beginning to wonder if there really could be somebody out there for me."

Christy smiled at her freckled-face, clear-eyed friend. "I'm sure there is. You will be a treasure for any guy to discover."

"Thanks for the vote of confidence, Christy. I guess I should just be patient and see what God has in mind, right?"

Christy nodded. But her thoughts were rapidly traveling back in time.

"Hello in there," Sierra said, waving her hand in front of Christy's face. "Where did you go?"

"Oh, I was just thinking about last summer. My family went camping, and we were hiking along this mountain trail that cut through the middle of a forest. My dad was next to me, and he held out his arm for me to hold on to while we walked down this path that was shaded by a canopy of huge trees."

Christy glanced over her shoulder to make sure no one else was listening. She leaned a little closer to Sierra and continued her story. "My dad comes across kind of gruff most of the time, but every now and then his tender side shows through, and he does or says things that just level me emotionally. So here we are, parading arm in arm down this trail, and he says, 'One day I'll be walking like this down the church aisle, and I'll be giving you away.' "

Sierra's eyes opened wide. "What did you do? I would have started to cry right there."

"Well, I almost did. It was so incredibly tender, the way his voice came out all rough and whispery at the same time. And then he said, 'Christina, I know you'll be wearing white on that day. I'll never be able to tell you how proud I am of you.' " Christy blinked away a tear and said, "And then from out of nowhere there came this wind that made all the trees start to shake their leaves. You know how it can sound like applause?"

"I know; I love that sound," Sierra said. "It's like that verse about all the trees in the field clapping their hands for joy."

Christy nodded. "Then my dad said, 'You're surrounded by a crowd of witnesses, Christy. Just listen.' So we stood there together, arm in arm, listening to the wind in the trees. Then my dad said, 'They're clapping for you, honey. They know a true princess when they see one.' "

Now Christy and Sierra were both crying, with slow, silent tears rolling down their cheeks.

"I am so glad I've been saving myself for my future husband," Sierra said softly. "That is, if there *is* a future husband for me somewhere. The peer pressure is for such a short time. And being married is like . . ." Sierra paused, searching for the right word.

"Forever," Christy said.

"Yeah. Forever."

CHAPTER ELEVEN

Missionary Woman

When Christy and her other teammates arrived back at Carnforth Hall at the end of their outreach, they joined all the other teams in the chapel. Even though it was late, everyone was wide awake, enthusiastically sharing stories of what God had done that day. The room seemed electrified with excitement as, for more than an hour, the team members took turns sharing their stories with the whole group.

They could have gone on for another hour, but Dr. Benson stepped in and closed the meeting by giving final details of when each of the teams was leaving for its ministry destination. Some were scheduled to depart in the morning because they had a longer distance to travel. The Belfast team wasn't leaving until later in the day. Their train ride would take them to Stranraer, where they would board the Sea Cat, a modern, high-speed ferry that would take them directly into Belfast Harbor at six o'clock that evening.

"You'll be met by the Reverend Norman Hutchins and his wife, Ruby." Dr. Benson read from his list while Doug quickly wrote down the names. "They have received a fax from us with your photo, Doug, so they'll be looking for you."

Dr. Benson went on to the next team and read their itinerary. Christy thought perhaps she should have written down some of the details for their trip. All she remembered was that they had to be ready to leave Carnforth Hall at eleven o'clock. From there, she could rely on Doug to lead them to Belfast.

As the meeting drew to a close, Christy's new friends from Finland, Merja and Satu, came over to say good-bye. "Our group leaves for Barcelona at four o'clock in the morning, so we had better say good-bye now. We're so glad we met you."

"Me too," Christy said, returning both their hugs. "Have a great time in Barcelona, and I'll see you back here for the last two days of the conference."

All over the chapel, people were hugging, laughing, crying. Some were gathered in small groups, holding hands and praying for each other. Christy felt sure God was about to do something incredible with each group.

The next morning breakfast was served at seven o'clock. Christy thought it seemed noticeably quieter in the dining room since two of the teams had already left. The Amsterdam team was scheduled to depart right after breakfast. Christy and Sierra had their suitcases packed and were ready to go.

Just as Christy took her last spoonful of porridge, Dr. Benson walked into the dining room and scanned the students' faces until his gaze rested on Christy's. He strode over to her and said, "May I speak with you a moment in my office?"

"Sure." Christy gave Katie and Sierra a shrug of her shoulders and followed him out the door. She couldn't help but feel she was in trouble. Or worse, what if it was bad news about something at home, like Avril's call?

"Is everything okay?" Christy asked as soon as she was seated in the chair in front of his huge wooden desk.

Dr. Benson took his seat and picked up some papers from his desk, which Christy recognized as her application. "Yes, I'd simply like to ask you a few questions."

Christy swallowed, and a bit of oatmeal caught in her throat. She began to cough.

"It says here that you speak Spanish."

Christy nodded and tried to stop her cough. "I . . . I took it for four years in high school." She kept coughing. "But I'm not fluent." The irritating tickle continued.

Dr. Benson rose and poured her a drink of water from a glass carafe sitting on the window sill. "Are you all right, then?"

Christy quickly drank the water, cleared her throat, and said, "Yes, I'm fine now. Thanks."

Dr. Benson continued. "We had an excellent report from Reverend Allistar regarding the children's ministry you led at his church on Saturday. You also have a glowing reference here from the children's ministry director at your home church." Placing the papers on his desk and leaning back in his chair, Dr. Benson said, "Let me come to the point. Perhaps you remember Avril, the young woman who went home last week."

"Yes. I heard her brother is out of the hospital and doing well," Christy said.

"He is, and that is good news. However, Avril has decided to stay home and not participate in the outreach. We completely understand her decision. Our dilemma is that Avril was our children's ministry worker on the Barcelona team."

"Oh," said Christy.

"There's more. Just this morning we received a fax from our missionary in Barcelona that their full-time children's worker had to return to the States. So as you can see, Barcelona is in great need of someone to do the children's ministry, particularly someone who is capable and who has a Spanish background."

Christy wasn't sure what he was getting at until Dr. Benson said, "What I'm asking, Christy, is are you willing to go to Barcelona?"

"Me?"

"Yes," he said. "You're the most qualified. It's up to you, though. Are you willing to trust God in this new way?"

"I . . . don't know. Didn't the Barcelona team already leave this morning?"

"Yes. What we would do is put you on the train with the Amsterdam team. You would travel with them as far as France and then take the train by yourself to Barcelona."

"By myself?"

Dr. Benson smiled. "The Lord will be with you. This is why I'm asking if you're willing to trust God in a new way."

Christy had never expected this. They were asking her to leave all her friends and travel alone to a place she wasn't prepared for and, from the sounds of it, single-handedly carry on the children's ministry. The only comforting thought was that Satu and Merja were on the Barcelona team. Certainly they would help her out.

"I don't know. Is it up to me to decide?"

"Yes, completely. I wish we had more time, but the Amsterdam team is leaving in . . ." he checked his watch, ". . . about ten minutes, and we would like you to travel with them as far as Calais."

"Calais? Where's that?"

"France." Dr. Benson picked up a fax and read the schedule. "You'll change trains at Calais and take an overnight train to Port Bou. We'll arrange for you to have a sleeper car so you'll be quite safe and comfortable. You will arrive in Port Bou on the Spanish side of the border at 11:02 the next morning and change trains to Barcelona at 12:25. You will arrive at Sants, the main train station in Barcelona, at 2:55 that afternoon. From there you'll take a commuter train at 3:15 and arrive at Playa Castelldefels at 3:30. It's really a lovely ride down the Costa Brava.''

Christy bowed her head, closed her eyes, and pursed her lips. Perhaps Dr. Benson thought she was praying. She was really trying hard not to cry. It all hit her so hard and fast. His rapid-fire itinerary seemed overwhelming. Plus this was her worst nightmare, having to make split-second decisions that might affect the rest of her life.

She knew the need was great, but what about Belfast? Gernot and the others could carry on in her absence, she supposed. Still, how could she change directions so instantly and go to Barcelona instead of Belfast? She had already written her parents and told them she was going to Belfast.

''Would I be doing the same lessons I prepared for Belfast?'' she asked, stalling for time.

''Yes, everything from your training will be exactly the same. They already have the craft materials and puppets with them. You'll be in a small town outside Barcelona, right on the Mediterranean coast and working with our local missionary. It's much warmer there than in Belfast.''

Christy wondered if he actually thought the weather would make a difference in her decision. It wasn't the weather; it was the insecurity of leaving her friends and doing something on her own. And the panic of having only a few seconds to decide.

''Okay, I'll go,'' Christy heard herself blurt out. For a moment she thought it was someone else's voice. Then, as if to make sure she heard herself right, she repeated, ''I'll go to Barcelona.''

''Wonderful!'' Dr. Benson said with a huge smile. ''The Lord will bless your devoted service to Him. This is the essence of genuine missionary work and separates the spectators from the true servants. You have the kind of heart God can use to accomplish great things for His kingdom!"

Christy wished she felt as brave as he made her sound. Before she realized what was happening, a stack of papers was thrust into her hand, and Dr. Benson was explaining how she was to go about buying her tickets when she arrived at Victoria Station in London.

Suddenly she wished she had said no. How could she remember all these details and manage to change trains by herself? She had depended on Doug during the rest of this trip to direct her to the right bus and train.

Maybe this was part of what God wanted to teach her, to be completely independent from any guy—or any human, for that matter—and to trust God alone.

She didn't have time to think of all the reasons for this crazy twist. All she knew was that in less than ten minutes, she had to get all her luggage downstairs and find a way to say good-bye to Katie, Doug, Tracy, Sierra, and the rest of her team.

Christy rose to leave.

Dr. Benson shook her hand warmly and said, "We'll fax your file to the mission director in Castelldefels. Your photo is on here, so he'll know who to look for at the station. It's a very small station. I'm sure you two will have no difficulty in finding each other. You know how Americans tend to stand out in a crowd."

Christy's head was spinning with details as she clutched her papers in her hand and, with weak knees, hurried up to her room.

I'm going to Spain. All by myself. I can't believe this is happening. And I won't even arrive there until tomorrow afternoon!

Seven minutes later, Christy stood in front of the two

Carnforth Hall vans, which were being loaded with the Amsterdam team's luggage.

"Good-bye," Tracy said, hugging Christy. "I love you. I'll be praying for you. You'll never know how much this past week with you has meant to me."

"I love you too," Christy said to Tracy.

"Okay, my turn to freak out, here," Katie said, giving Christy a quick hug and trying hard to keep the tears in her green eyes from spilling over. "Can I just say one thing?"

Christy had to smile. Katie always used that line, but she always had more than one thing to say.

Katie struck her buff muscle-man pose and spouted, "You are missionary woman!"

They all laughed, which made it easier for Christy to hug Gernot, Ian, and Stephen. But then it was Doug's turn, and she felt herself choking up.

"You're awesome, Christy," he said, wrapping his arms around her in one of his super hugs. "God is awesome. He's going to do awesome things in your life. Thanks for everything. Really. Thanks."

He squeezed her in another hug, and she whispered in his ear, "You're welcome, Sir Honesty. Take care of your princess."

Doug pulled away and smiled at her. "I will," he said. "Thanks, Christy."

Sierra was the last to say good-bye. "I don't know why I'm crying. I'm going to see you again in just a little more than a week when we meet back here." She hugged Christy and said, "I just feel like we really connected, you know? I wish we could have stayed together."

"I know," Christy said. "Me, too. You can come to Barcelona with me if you want." Christy playfully grabbed Sierra by the arm and pretended to push her into the van.

"Hey, wait a minute," Katie said. "Red rover, red rover, send Sierra back over!"

Doug said, "Losing you, Christy, is about as much of a sacrifice as anyone should have to make in one week."

Christy thought his words carried an underlying message aimed at their breaking up. That made it even harder for her to leave. She thought of how close their team had become after their week of training. God had answered her prayers for unity, and now they were becoming divided by her leaving. It didn't make sense.

Katie's phrase echoed in her mind: "God is weird."

"Time to go," the van driver called as he started up the engine.

Forcing a smile, Christy waved to her old teammates and climbed into the van. "Bye. I'll be praying for you guys. Pray for me!"

The van door slid shut, and Christy's seven friends all stood in a line, waving good-bye. Then at Katie's signal, just as the van pulled away, all seven of them assumed a weight-lifter pose and called out, "You are missionary woman!"

She laughed aloud, and one of the guys in the van said, "What was that?"

"A little joke," Christy said, still wavering between smiling and crying.

The train ride to London seemed to go quickly. Christy sat beside Jakobs, the guy from Latvia Katie had introduced her to. Jakobs was several years younger than Christy, but in some ways he seemed more mature, as if he had lived more of life in his sixteen years than Christy would experience in a lifetime. Jakobs wore his very short hair brushed straight up in the front. He was a few inches shorter than Christy.

Several hours into their train ride, Jakobs bought Christy a cup of tea and shared some of his sack lunch with her. Mrs. Bates had handed each of the students a sack lunch and at the same time had promptly planted a kiss on every team member's right cheek. Christy had stuck her lunch into an open corner of her suitcase, which was now nearly impossible to get at. She gladly shared Jakobs's sandwich.

"Are you yet used to the idea of going to Spain?" Jakobs asked.

Something mechanical turned on inside Christy's head, and she said, "Yes, I believe this is God's plan, and so I know He will work everything out. I'm learning to trust God in new ways."

A slow grin crept up Jakobs's face. "I think you are speaking to me through the flowers."

Although Jakobs's English was very good, sometimes his accent made his words sound a little unclear to Christy. She asked what he meant by "speaking through the flowers."

Jakobs looked a bit embarrassed. "It's an expression from where I live in Riga. We use it to mean when a person is making a pretty covering for his words and not saying what he truly feels. You are then 'speaking to me through the flowers.' "

Christy knew Jakobs was right. She was trying to sound brave and spiritual. What she really felt was terrified. Did she dare tell him? He seemed the sort of person she could trust.

"I'm really scared," she said.

Jakobs gave her a look of compassion and said, "Of what?"

"Of getting lost. Of missing my train connections."

"Then you can take the next train," Jakobs answered logically.

"But what if I can't find the right train? What if something happens, and I lose my luggage or my passport?"

"You go to your Embassy, apply for another passport, and wear your same clothes for two days in a row."

Christy couldn't tell if Jakobs was teasing her or if he was trying to be helpful. Earlier that week Christy had overheard Jakobs talking with a Texan about how Americans were overly concerned about their clothes and hygiene. The girl from Texas had to wash and blow-dry her hair every morning, and she never went out in public without her makeup perfectly applied. Jakobs told her she should try wearing the same clothes for more than one day to practice being a good steward of what God had given her. The girl told Jakobs he was crazy.

Christy didn't think he was crazy, but she did think he had a rather simplistic approach to life. "What if I get attacked, or what if I get killed?" Christy said, challenging him with a worst-possible scenario.

Jakobs's grin returned, and he said, "Then you will die and be with the Lord, and perhaps I might envy you getting to heaven before me."

Christy smiled back. Jakobs certainly had an eternal perspective on life. With such heaven-oriented thinking, it made it hard to see anything as bad. In Jakobs's vocabulary, the term "tragedy" didn't seem to exist.

Christy finished her last sip of lukewarm tea and said, "In America we would probably call you a 'Pollyanna.' That means someone who finds the good in every situation."

"In Riga, you would probably tell me to 'find ducks,' " Jakobs said and then chuckled at his own apparent joke.

" 'Find ducks'?" Christy asked.

"It's our way of saying 'go away.' Not everyone says it. Just some of my friends. If you go to Riga, you might not want to try that on just anyone. Especially someone like the officer who stamps your visa."

Christy couldn't begin to imagine what it would be like to visit a country like Latvia. Spain was exotic enough for her.

Spain. The sudden thought of Spain paralyzed her all over again. Her feelings must have shown on her face.

"Are you again worried about the trains?" Jakobs asked.

Christy knew better than to try "speaking through the flowers" to him again. "I guess a little."

"What is your verse?" Jakobs asked.

"My verse?"

"You need a verse. Something from God's Word to plant in your heart for this trip."

"To plant in the garden of my heart?" Christy said, thinking of Tracy's poem.

"Yes. You need a promise to . . . how do you say it?" Jakobs clenched his fist. "Held on with?"

"You mean to hold on to," Christy said. "You think I need a special verse to hold on to."

"Yes, I do."

"Do you have a verse?" Christy asked.

Jakobs nodded, and he rattled off some words in his melodic Latvian tongue. "It is Jeremiah 1·7–8. Sorry, but I do not yet know it in English. May I read it in your Bible?"

Christy dug to the bottom of her bag, pulled out her Bible, and turned to Jakobs's verse. She handed her Bible to him, and in his wonderful accent he read it to her. " 'But the LORD said to me, "Do not say, 'I am only a child.' You must go to everyone I send you to and say whatever I command you. Do not be afraid of them, for I am with you and will rescue you," declares the LORD.' "

"That's perfect!" Christy said. "That's exactly how I feel."

"This is my verse," Jakobs said in a teasing voice, holding Christy's Bible close to his chest. "You need to search until you find your own verse."

"Oh, go find ducks!" Christy said, teasing him right back. "I can have the same verse if I want to. Now give me my Bible back!"

Jakobs laughed and said, "You should do just fine in your new culture. I am not worried for you at all."

Christy hoped Jakobs's words would come true. They seemed true enough when the group made its connection in London. Everything went as planned, nice and smooth. All Christy had to do was follow the other team members to the ticket window and buy her ticket to cross the English Channel. Then she waited in line with them again to buy her train ticket to Barcelona while the others bought their tickets to Amsterdam.

The envelope Dr. Benson had handed her that morning had a little money left over after the purchase of her tickets. With the two pounds and some change, Christy bought herself a candy bar while they waited.

Fortunately, she decided against eating it right away. The ferry ride across the English Channel proved to be a little too rough for her stomach. The candy bar would have come right back up.

About twenty-five minutes into the trip, Christy knew she couldn't postpone the inevitable any longer. Leaving her seat next to Jakobs, she cautiously maneuvered her way to the bathroom. She barely made it into one of the bathroom stalls before she threw up. She hated throwing up. What made it worse was, right when she thought she might be okay, she could hear someone in the stall next to her throwing up, and that made her feel like doing it all over again.

It was a horrible experience. Christy slumped on the

bathroom floor, feeling too weak to return to her seat.

This is awful; I'm never going to make it. I can't go on! This whole trip was a huge mistake. God, what are you trying to do to me?

Another overwhelming urge to throw up seized her, and she stumbled to the sink, where her stomach muscles went through their wrenching motions, but she had nothing else to throw up. Rinsing out her mouth and wetting a paper towel to hold against her throbbing head, Christy sank again to the floor next to another sick passenger.

Under her breath she groaned, "I am *not* missionary woman."

CHAPTER TWELVE

Midnight Picnic

When they arrived in Calais at 6:30 that night, Christy felt as if she could barely walk. Her head pounded, her throat felt raw and clenched, and she was desperate for a drink of cold water. One of the guys on the Amsterdam team watched their baggage while Christy, with the sympathetic assistance of Jakobs, who also had gotten seasick, went in search of a snack bar and some bottled water.

Everything moved in slow motion as Christy and Jakobs had to exchange money, stand in line to pay an outrageous price for the bottles of water, and then find the rest of the group. Christy collapsed onto a bench where the rest of the team had gathered with their luggage and slowly sipped her water. Overhead, train departure times were being announced in French and several other languages. From where Christy sat, she could see a large board that listed train schedules with their departure times.

"We need to get all our luggage to that track down there," the Amsterdam team captain told Christy as their group began to pick out their luggage from the pile next to the bench. "Will you be okay here, Christy?"

She wanted to scream out, "No, don't leave me!" The only

words she mustered were "I'm not sure which track my train leaves from."

"I'm sure you can figure it out," the guy said. He didn't say it in an unkind way; it was just that he obviously had his hands full with four of his team members also feeling sick and their train leaving in less than fifteen minutes. "Just look on that sign over there for the 8:24 overnight train to Port Bou. It can't be that hard. Or ask someone."

With a round of hurried good-byes and a warm handshake from Jakobs, the Amsterdam team moved away like a row of ducks to their train track. Jakobs was about twenty yards away from her when he turned around and called out, "Don't forget to find your verse!" He still looked a little green around the gills and appeared to be using a lot of strength to yell his encouragement to her.

Christy sat still. All around her spun a busy, loud confusion of travelers. She felt cold, and the station suddenly smelled like mildew. Or maybe it was her breath that smelled so bad. Christy tried another swig of water, and then, popping out the handle on her wheeled suitcase, she gathered all her belongings and headed toward the train schedule board, as if she knew exactly what she was doing.

There it was plain as day, the name "Port Bou," and the time listed next to it was "8:24." Track three. How hard had that been? Now where was track three?

Christy had nearly half an hour before the train departed, but she wanted to find the right track. Walking seemed to help her recover from her seasickness, especially since the ground was level and didn't move under her feet the way it had during the English Channel crossing. The ferry ride had taken all afternoon, and although it was the cheapest way to get to France, it certainly didn't seem to Christy to be the best way. Maybe she could persuade the mission director in Barcelona to allow her to personally pay the extra amount, whatever it was, to fly back to England instead of repeating this train and ferry trip.

When she arrived at track three, there was no train. But several people were standing around. They seemed to be waiting, so she thought she must be in the right place.

Rolling her luggage and toting her black shoulder bag over to a vacant spot on a nearby bench, Christy felt as if she were going to faint. Everything in front of her began to get dark, and her vision narrowed to a small circle of bright spinning dots. She sat down just in time.

After she lowered her head and breathed deeply, everything came back into focus. Christy drank some more water and tried to get her pounding heart to slow to a steady pace.

Everything's okay. You can do this. The Lord is with you.

Christy had never thought of herself as a weak person. She hated this sensation of losing control. She wanted everything to be normal and calm and right up front where she could see it. She wanted to feel strong and in control again, and yet she couldn't. All she felt was queasy and weak and as if she were barely hanging on with her fingernails.

Just then she heard the loud rumble of her train coming down the track. It even drowned out the sound of the French announcer's voice over the loudspeaker.

Christy reached for her ticket in her bag. It wasn't there. She fumbled through all her junk and couldn't find it. Then, unzipping the bag's side pouch, Christy plunged her hand in. Right next to her butane curling iron, she felt the reassuring forms of her passport and her train ticket.

Don't panic, Christy! Whatever you do, don't freak out here. You're doing fine.

Christy was one of the first passengers to board the train. The conductor in a black coat and hat looked at her ticket as she stepped up into the train. He rattled off something to her in French.

"What? I'm sorry. I don't understand you," she said.

The man motioned with his hand toward the back of the train as a stream of French words tumbled from his mouth. "Ze sleeper cars are in ze back of ze train," a woman behind Christy said. She didn't look up at Christy, and she hadn't spoken very loudly—just enough for Christy to hear and understand.

"Oh, I'm sorry. Thank you. Excuse me." Christy tried to turn around on the narrow landing and go down the steps back to the train platform. Her suitcase got caught in the small space, and Christy couldn't budge it. The conductor spoke harshly to her again in French. She used all her might to free the snagged suitcase and get down the steps.

Once on the platform, Christy walked as fast as her wobbly legs would take her to the far end of the train. There she tried to enter the train again with the assistance of another conductor. He looked at her ticket and pointed the other way, toward the front of the train, speaking briskly in French.

"But I just came from there, and they sent me down here!" She felt sure the man could understand her, even though he waved his hand and spoke back to her in French.

Before she could stop them, salty tears filled her eyes, and she felt all the color drain from her face. "Could you please help me?" she said to the conductor.

He looked at her again, and his expression softened a bit. Motioning for her to enter the train, he lifted her suitcase for her and indicated that she should follow him. He lead the way through several train cars that were all linked together, down the narrow hallway of the train lined with windows on one side and compartments with closed doors on the other. Suddenly he stopped in front of a compartment and slid open the door, indicating for her to enter.

"Thank you," Christy said, viewing the empty compartment with the two upholstered bench seats that faced each other. She couldn't wait to lie down and get some sleep.

The conductor entered the small compartment with her and lifted her suitcase to an overhead rack. Then, with a tug on one of the seats, he pulled it out to reveal a sort of Hide-a-Bed already made up. He reached for a blanket from the overhead rack and muttered a few more French words.

Christy thought to reach for some money to tip him. She grabbed everything she had in her coat pocket left over from when she and Jakobs had bought the water. She had no idea if the handful of francs she offered him was a lot or a little.

He glanced at the bills and coins she had dropped into his hand and then looked again. With a tip of his hat he backed out of her train compartment and mumbled something in French.

Christy pulled the shades down on her compartment windows that faced the narrow hallway and then closed the shade on the large window that overlooked the train tracks and the station. Her bed looked so inviting. Slipping off her shoes and pulling back the covers, Christy crawled in and hoped to sleep straight through until the morning light peeked in.

She fell into a deep sleep as the train pulled out of the station, rocking her with its rhythmic motion down the tracks. Unfortunately her sleep lasted only a short time. Someone suddenly slid her compartment door open, spoke loudly in French, and snapped on the overhead light.

It was a conductor, but not the one who had helped her earlier. *"Passporte,"* he said. Then in exaggerated English, "Passport."

Christy groped for her shoulder bag, which she had tucked under the covers with her as a precaution. She handed him her passport and ticket. He looked it over, seemed satisfied, and jammed the sliding door shut as abruptly as he had opened it. The rude fellow had left on the light.

Christy returned her passport to its safe place in her bag and then crawled out of her burrow to turn off the light. The train slowed to a stop. Apparently they were at another station. A few minutes later the train started up again. The voices of new passengers could be heard in the hallway outside her door. Now Christy couldn't get back to sleep.

At least she felt better. She sat up in bed and finished her bottle of water. Then she realized how hungry she was. It was nearly midnight, and she hadn't eaten for close to twelve hours. Snapping the light back on, she scrounged through her suitcase until she found the sack lunch Mrs. Bates had packed for her. Sitting cross-legged, Christy spread her little picnic out on her bed, folded her hands, and bowed her head to pray.

"It's just You and me, Lord. Thank You for taking care of me and for providing this food for our little midnight picnic. Thanks for making me feel better. I'm sorry I blamed You for this trip back on the ferry. I just hate being sick."

Christy opened her eyes and took a bite of her sandwich, but she continued talking to Jesus as if He were sitting next to her. "I just like everything to be, well . . . comfortable. I guess I like to be in control. But, then, that's supposed to be Your job, isn't it?"

It hit her like a revelation. She pictured herself standing by the gate of her heart's garden. Jesus was definitely in the garden with her, but clearly Christy was the one who held the key to the gate.

She put down her sandwich, and looking into the thin air next to her, she said, "That's what's been missing, huh? I'm still the one making all the decisions, holding the key, and I'm the one deciding who should come in and out of my garden. I've been the one locking and unlocking the gate. I've been the one in control.

"Lord Jesus," Christy whispered, "I want You to hold the key. I want You to decide what should happen in my heart's garden. I want You to let in or send out anything or anybody You want. Especially with guys. I don't want to ever unlock that gate again. I want You to open it only when the right man comes along. Take the key, Lord. Take all my keys. I'll wait for You."

For a moment Christy thought she might be going crazy because a sweet fragrance seemed to be in the cabin after she prayed. Certainly in her heart's garden there was the fragrance of fresh, blooming newness. She felt so free, so completely right with God. She continued their picnic, imagining that she and Jesus were seated together under a plumeria tree in her heart's garden. Beside them a wild patch of daffodils bobbed their heads and a long, trailing vine of jasmine lined the trellis that covered her garden gate.

Christy couldn't remember the last time she had felt so happy. So safe. So completely content. She had never felt this close to Jesus, either.

"Is it because there's always been some guy in my garden with me? Is that why I've never before been so open and sought You so wholeheartedly?" Christy wondered aloud. "I want it to be You and me, Lord. Always. Close, like this. Even if You do bring a guy into my life, I still want to feel this close to You. Forever."

So many things seemed to make sense to Christy. The unsettled feelings she had fought with last week were gone. She knew the weeks ahead of her would be difficult and stretching, yet she wasn't afraid of what might happen. She felt tremendous assurance that she had done the right thing in letting go of Doug.

She even felt a peace about Todd. She had done the right thing in letting him go too. He was serving God, and that was where he belonged. Christy knew she needed to move on, to fully become the woman God created her to be and not to be dependent on any guy. She would be dependent on the Lord alone.

After eating half her sandwich and two of her carrot sticks, Christy put away her lunch, deciding to save the rest for later. It was the middle of the night, and she desperately needed some sleep.

Turning off the light, she thought of one of the evening verses Dr. Benson had quoted, "I will lie down and sleep in peace, for you alone, O LORD, make me dwell in safety."

"Amen," she whispered, and she fell into a deep sleep.

But not for long.

CHAPTER THIRTEEN

Forever

Suddenly the door of Christy's compartment flew open, and a rough, coarse voice blared into the darkness.

"Who's there?" Christy called out, sitting up in bed.

The overhead light flipped on, temporarily blinding her with its flash.

"What do you want?" Christy demanded of the gruff, smelly, obviously drunk man who had entered her compartment. "Get out of here," she yelled. "I mean it! Get out of here right now, or I'll scream."

The confused man stumbled farther into her room, and the door slid shut behind him. As it did, Christy let out the loudest scream she could.

The man covered his ears but didn't move. Christy screamed again, then drew in a deeper breath and screamed again. The door slid open, and two conductors and three passengers all crammed inside, grabbing the man by the arm and ushering him out as quickly as he had found his way in.

The conductor who had helped Christy find her room now stood beside her and in a soothing voice spoke to her in French. She scrambled to remember the word for "thank you" and hoarsely told the conductor, *"Merci."*

He kept talking and pointed to her door. She thought at first he wanted her to leave, and she began to get out of bed. He motioned for her to stay, and then he went out the door. Christy waited a moment and then peeked out the drawn shades into the hallway. The conductor was still standing by her door. Apparently he had appointed himself her personal bodyguard for the remainder of her trip through France.

I must have tipped him a lot of money, Christy thought. *Either that, or he's my guardian angel in disguise.*

She swallowed; her throat hurt terribly. She found a cough drop in her bag and tried to sleep. It was an on-and-off endeavor.

Right before sunrise, Christy decided she couldn't wait any longer to go to the bathroom. She put on her shoes and looped her black bag over her arm. Carefully opening her door, she was almost surprised to see that her personal guard wasn't standing there.

Then Christy heard a *"bonjour"* and saw that he had moved to the end of the hallway and was smoking a cigarette by an open window.

Probably not my guardian angel. She smiled, said *"Merci"* again, and pointed to the tiny train rest room across the way. When she came out several minutes later, the conductor was still standing there. He pointed to something out the window, and she stopped to see the sun coming up across rolling green hills. An old stone barn stood alone in the distance. The chilly wind from the open window blew her hair back. It was a beautiful scene and a beautiful morning. Christy imagined they must be somewhere in the middle of France, but she had no idea where.

Back in her compartment, she crawled into her warm bed. She lifted the shade on her window just far enough to see outside. For nearly an hour she sat contentedly watching the breathtaking scenery roll past her.

"I'd like to come back someday," she said to her Silent Companion. "I'd like to explore every little village we've passed and experience all kinds of new adventures."

Christy pulled out her journal and recorded the events of the past few days as best she could. It seemed impossible that so much had happened in such a short time.

After bringing her journal entries up to the event of the drunken man and her uniformed bodyguard, Christy wrote, *I think I know what I'd like to be when I grow up. Or should I say, what I think God would like me to be when I grow up. I'd like to be a missionary. Here, in Europe. I like working with children. Surely there's some place that needs a missionary to tell the little kids about Jesus. Whatever it takes in schooling or training, I want to go after it wholeheartedly when I get home.*

Reaching for her sack lunch, Christy opened her bottle of orange juice. She sat back, enjoyed the scenery, drank orange juice, and ate the Toblerone candy bar she had bought before the ferry ride.

The memory of that nightmare of a trip made her shudder. At the same time, she felt as if she had accomplished something grand and glorious. She had made it this far in one piece. She felt she could do anything.

The renewed energy and confidence came in handy at Port Bou when she had to change trains. The train to Barcelona left Port Bou promptly at 12:25. It was an older train and much more crowded. Christy didn't have a compartment to herself, but shared it with five other people. Two women who appeared to be traveling together sat across from Christy and spoke such rapid Spanish that Christy could barely understand what they were saying. A teenage boy sat next to her, reading a paperback book. An elderly woman sat next to him and talked to another woman seated across from her until they both nodded off.

It felt peculiar to share a compartment with these strangers until Christy realized they were ignoring her. Perhaps she shouldn't be so interested in them. This would be a good time to finish her sandwich and the apple left in her lunch.

With her first bite into the sandwich, Christy thought of Jakobs, who had shared his sandwich with her. She wondered if he had gone hungry later in his journey to Amsterdam. Then she remembered his words at the Calais train station about finding her own verse.

She pulled out her Bible and began to skim through the psalms to see if she had underlined any verses that would mean a lot to her now. Every verse she read touched her in a different way. She had never felt so refreshed reading her Bible.

After nearly an hour, Christy found a verse that seemed perfect for her desire to be a missionary and to work with children. She copied Psalm 78:4 into her diary: *"We will not hide them from their children; we will tell the next generation the praiseworthy deeds of the* LORD, *his power, and the wonders he has done."*

That verse stirred within Christy a call to serve God, yet it didn't seem like "her" verse, the way Jakobs's had seemed so personal for him. So she read on.

And then, in Psalm 86:11 and 12, she found it. *"Teach me your way, O* LORD, *and I will walk in your truth; give me an undivided heart, that I may fear your name. I will praise you, O* LORD *my God, with all my heart; I will glorify your name forever."*

"Forever," Christy repeated as she wrote the last word in her journal. "With all my heart forever," she whispered. It felt as if the Lord were sitting right next to her, listening to every word of her promise.

When she heard an audible voice next to her, she jumped.

"Pardon me. May I ask what you are reading?" It was the teenage boy. Christy had thought he was sleeping. To her surprise she realized he had been observing her, and he spoke English.

"It's a Bible," Christy said.

"Do you mean the Holy Bible?" he asked, eyeing her Bible. Perhaps the pink-flowered fabric cover seemed unusual to him.

"Yes, of course. The Bible."

He looked surprised. "And you have been reading it this long? And with such interest?"

Christy nodded. "Do you ever read the Bible?"

"No," the tanned, dark-haired boy said, "I do not have one."

Without thinking, Christy said, "Here, would you like to have mine?"

His eyes grew wide in disbelief.

Christy quickly removed the pink cover. "Really. You can have it. It's in English, but you seem to speak English very well." She placed the Bible in his hand and said, "Here. I want you to have it, really."

"*Muchas gracias*. Thank you."

"You have to read it now," she said with a smile. She was thinking of the teenage boy in England who had scoffed at her after the drama performance.

"I will. Thank you."

"Are you going to Barcelona?" Christy asked.

"Yes," the boy answered, "I surf there sometimes. Sitges has better surfing, though. It's not far."

Surfing, Christy thought. *Maybe I will feel at home here*.

"This is Sants now," the boy said as the train began to slow down in a huge station. "You will change here. The train to Cas-telldefels is very nice. More modern. Go to platform five and get on the Villa Nova train."

"Thank you," Christy said. "By the way, my name is Christy. What's your name?"

"Carlos."

"I'm working with a group of people in Castelldefels who are doing drama and music this week," Christy said. "Maybe you can come sometime, Carlos. I'm sorry I don't know when or where it will be."

"Castelldefels is not a very big place," he said with a smile. "I should be able to find you. Thank you again for your Bible. You are a different woman."

As soon as Christy was situated on the modern commuter train, she reviewed Carlos's words in her mind. *"You are a different woman."* She supposed "different" was meant in a good way. And he had said woman, not girl. Maybe she had grown up so much on this trip that it showed—even to strangers.

Christy could picture herself relating this story to Katie when they gathered back at Carnforth Hall. She would flex her arms and tell Katie, "I am different woman!" Indeed, that's how she felt.

Christy glanced out the window and spotted the ocean. The Mediterranean Sea, to be exact. It was a beautiful, rich blue color. Suddenly she felt at home. She could almost smell the moist ocean air through the closed train windows. A smile grew as Christy thought of how it would feel in a few short minutes to take off her shoes and socks and wiggle her bare feet in the cool sand on the beach.

This is it, Lord! This is perfect. Thank You for bringing me here; I could stay forever.

Then it hit Christy that she had no idea who was meeting her at the station. Dr. Benson had said the mission director would have her photo along with her application. She decided to look for a man like Dr. Benson, late forties, hair graying by the temples and wearing . . . wearing what? A flowered surfing shirt? Christy giggled at the thought of a mission director who might know how to surf. For all she knew, this guy would greet her in a sombrero and riding a donkey! Hopefully Merja and Satu would be there too, and they would recognize her right away.

She felt nervous. This was it. She had made it all the way by herself. With the Lord, of course. But here she was. And in less than five minutes, the train would stop, and she would begin her week as a missionary woman.

She decided to make a quick run to the train's rest room and do her best to look presentable. It wasn't an easy task. The eighteen hours of travel had taken their toll on her. But a quick wash of her face and brush of her hair helped her to feel refreshed. She had a sample vial of perfume, which she snapped open and rubbed up and down her arms.

Much better. Now to get my luggage and stand by the door.

As soon as the train came to a stop, Christy jumped off, all smiles. She looked around. There was no Satu. No Merja. And no mission director on a donkey. She saw no one who even vaguely looked as if he might be waiting for her.

I thought this was the right place.

She glanced around the small, nearly vacant station. There was a ticket booth and what looked like a snack bar. The station itself was old and run-down.

The train pulled away, heading down the coast toward Sitges. Christy wistfully watched it go. That's when she noticed the graffiti on the wall, and with the ocean breeze racing through the corridor came the smell of urine.

Lord, remember me? What are we doing here?

All her courage left her. This had to be a mistake. Christy reached into her bag and fumbled for the papers Dr. Benson had given her. Perhaps there was a phone number to call. Was there even a pay phone around this place? And what could she use for money? She hadn't exchanged any traveler's checks into pesetas yet. Where were those papers?

Christy dug her hand deeper into her shoulder bag. Scanning the papers she finally located there, she found no phone numbers or addresses listed. All the plans had been made in such haste. All she knew was that someone was supposed to meet her. She was here and he or she wasn't.

Never in her life had she felt so completely alone. Stranded with nowhere to turn. A prayer came quickly to her lips. "Father God, I'm at Your mercy here. I know You're in control. Please show me what to do."

Suddenly she heard a voice calling to her.

"Kilikina!"

Christy's heart stopped. Only one person in the entire world had ever called her by her Hawaiian name. She spun around.

"Kilikina," called out the tall, blond surfer who was running toward her.

Christy looked up into the screaming silver-blue eyes that could only belong to one person.

"Todd?" she whispered, convinced she was hallucinating.

"Kilikina," Todd wrapped his arms around her so tightly that for an instant she couldn't breathe. He held her a long time. Crying. She could feel his warm tears on her neck. She knew this had to be real. But how could it be?

"Todd?" she whispered again. "How? I mean, what? . . . I don't . . ."

Todd pulled away, and for the first time she noticed the big bouquet of white carnations in his hand. They were now a bit squashed.

"For you," he said, his eyes clearing and his rich voice sounding calm and steady. Then, seeing her shocked expression, he asked, "You really didn't know I was here, did you?"

Christy shook her head, unable to find any words.

"Didn't Dr. Benson tell you?"

She shook her head again.

"You mean you came all this way by yourself, and you didn't even know I was here?" Now it was Todd's turn to look surprised.

"No, I thought you were in Papua New Guinea or something. I had no idea you were here!"

"They needed me here more," Todd said with a chin-up gesture toward the beach. "It's the perfect place for me." With a wide smile spreading above his square jaw, he said, "Ever since I received the fax yesterday saying they were sending you, I've been out of my mind with joy! Kilikina, you can't imagine how I've been feeling."

Christy had never heard him talk like this before.

Todd took the bouquet from her and placed it on top of her luggage. Then, grasping both her quivering hands in his and looking into her eyes, he said, "Don't you see? There is no way you or I could ever have planned this. It's from God."

The shocked tears finally caught up to Christy's eyes, and she blinked to keep Todd in focus. "It is," she agreed. "God brought us back together, didn't He?" A giggle of joy and delight danced from her lips.

"Do you remember what I said when you gave me back your

bracelet?" Todd asked. "I said that if God ever brought us back together, I would put that bracelet back on your wrist, and that time, it would stay on forever."

Christy nodded. She had replayed the memory of that day a thousand times in her mind. It had seemed impossible that God would bring them back together. Christy's heart pounded as she realized that God, in His weird way, had done the impossible.

Todd reached into his pocket and pulled out the "Forever" ID bracelet. He tenderly held Christy's wrist, and circling it with the gold chain, he secured the clasp.

Above their heads a fresh ocean wind blew through the palm trees. It almost sounded as if the trees were applauding.

Christy looked up from her wrist and met Todd's expectant gaze. Deep inside, Christy knew that with the blessing of the Lord, Todd had just stepped into the garden of her heart.

In the holiness of that moment, his silver-blue eyes embraced hers and he whispered, "I promise, Kilikina. Forever."

"Forever," Christy whispered back.

Then gently, reverently, Todd and Christy sealed their forever promise with a kiss.

Don't Miss These Captivating Stories in
THE CHRISTY MILLER SERIES

THE SIERRA JENSEN SERIES

If you've enjoyed reading about Christy Miller,
you'll love reading about Christy's friend Sierra Jensen.

#1 • Only You, Sierra
When her family moves to another state, Sierra dreads going to a new high school—until she meets Paul.

#2 • In Your Dreams
Just when events in Sierra's life start to look up—she even gets asked out on a date—Sierra runs into Paul.

#3 • Don't You Wish
Sierra is excited about visiting Christy Miller in California during Easter break. Unfortunately, her sister, Tawni, decides to go with her.

#4 • Close Your Eyes
Sierra experiences a sticky situation when Paul comes over for dinner and Randy shows up at the same time.

#5 • Without A Doubt
When handsome Drake reveals his interest in Sierra, life gets complicated.

#6 • With This Ring
Sierra couldn't be happier when she goes to Southern California to join Christy Miller and their friends for Doug and Tracy's wedding.

#7 • Open Your Heart
When Sierra's friend Christy Miller receives a scholarship from a university in Switzerland, she invites Sierra to go with her and Aunt Marti to visit the school.

#8 • Time Will Tell
After an exciting summer in Southern California and Switzerland, Sierra returns home to several unsettled relationships.

#9 • Now Picture This
When Sierra and Paul start corresponding, she imagines him as her boyfriend and soon begins neglecting her family and friends.

#10 • Hold On Tight
Sierra joins her brother and several friends on a road trip to Southern California to visit potential colleges.

#11 • Closer Than Ever
When Paul doesn't show up for her graduation party and news comes that a flight from London has crashed, Sierra frantically worries about the future.

#12 • Take My Hand
A costly misunderstanding leaves Sierra anxious as she says goodbye to Portland and heads off to California for her freshman year of college.

THE CHRISTY MILLER SERIES

12

forever

*Get acquainted with
Christy's friend
Sierra by reading all
twelve books in the*
S I E R R A
J E N S E N
S E R I E S,
*also by
Robin Jones Gunn.*

**BETHANY HOUSE
PUBLISHERS**
MINNEAPOLIS, MN 55438

US $6.99

ISBN 1-56179-733-2

9 781561 797332

DBR642636

A castle in the mist, a yearning
heart, and a lonely train ride all
teach Christy that...

*A
Promise
Is
Forever*

Off on a European mission trip with her
friends, Christy Miller discovers foreign
adventure is her cup of tea. She can just
see herself tromping through the streets
of London, traveling across different countries, and talking to new people, like her
new friend Sierra Jensen. But when ten-
sions among the group set in, Christy
finds memories of Todd, her past boyfriend, are constantly swimming in her
mind—no matter how hard she tries to
delete him from her mind!

To make matters worse, she is assigned
to go to Spain by herself while all her
friends travel elsewhere. Will Christy face
her fears of the future? And can she truly
trust that God has great things planned
for her even when all seems lost?

P9-CEW-019